ONE FINE FAE

MOLLY HARPER

One Fine Fae
Copyright © 2020 by Molly Harper
Ebook ISBN: 9781641971751
Print ISBN: 9798549345461

NYLA Publishing
121 W 27th St., Suite 1201, New York, NY 10001
http://www.nyliterary.com

1

CHARLOTTE

*C*harlotte McBee was accustomed to the incredulous looks she got while driving her over-sized airstream trailer down the highway. *Nobody* expected the Silver Stork. But had she known about the wedding taking place in Mystic Bayou's town square, she probably would have taken another route.

Charlotte slumped in the seat of her truck, practically folding her small frame into the space under the steering wheel as hundreds of eyes followed the Silver Stork's progress down Main Street.

It wasn't that Charlotte was embarrassed of her beautiful metal darling, but she'd seen enough wedding reality shows to know that distracting guests from the bride could end in violence. And Charlotte had been driving for too long to put up much of a fight.

Charlotte thought she could park near the League office complex, but then realized that the collection of temporary buildings that housed their offices *and* employees was on the opposite side of the square – directly behind the wedding party. So, she just eased down the street to the Mystic Bayou Parish Hall and parked across multiple spots.

The "town proper" was like so many rural small towns where she'd worked in her ten years as a midwife consulting for the International League for Interspecies Cooperation – one main street that included most of the town's businesses and municipal buildings branching out into a "tree" of residential streets with small one-level houses. She imagined that most of the locals lived in the dense swamplands that surrounded this tiny spot of civilization.

Charlotte hopped out of the truck, groaning in relief as she stretched her legs, short as they were. Most of the wedding guests seemed to have stopped staring and returned to their merriment. According to her official League welcome email, she was supposed to talk to an AJ Lancaster, the executive director of the League's operation here in town. She pulled her fancy satellite smart phone from her pocket, an essential when the League sent her to some of the most remote locations in the continental United States. She dialed Lancaster's cell phone number, but he didn't pick up.

She glanced up and down Main Street, wondering whether there was some place she could grab something to eat. Most of the businesses, small single-story, cement block affairs, seemed to be owned by a "Boone." The local bank, a boat dealership, the grocery store, the beauty salon, the hardware store – all of their signs practically shouted "Boone," The only eateries seemed to be a gray and navy building called The Ice Cream Depot, and "Bathtilda's Pie Shop, Home of the World's Best Chocolate Rhubarb Pie," both of which were closed.

She paused, chewing her lip in disappointed distress. After a long day of driving, she'd really been looking forward to something that she hadn't cobbled together herself in her kitchenette. And it didn't help that the wedding party seemed to center around some sort of meat-laden firepit. The smoke wafting across the square smelled like absolute heaven.

"Hello!"

Charlotte turned to see a man in a dark bespoke suit, all broad shoulders and dark blond hair, walking briskly towards her. He looked like a central casting version of an upwardly mobile prosecutor. She hoped desperately that she hadn't violated some archaic local parking law. She didn't have time to serve in the local ... wait, did they have a local jail here? She didn't see one.

"Hi, there, are you Charlotte McBee, by any chance?" Mr. Upwardly Mobile asked, extending his hand for a shake.

"I am," Charlotte said.

The man grinned broadly. "I'm Alex Lancaster, generally known as AJ Lancaster on my stationery. The head office said you'd wrapped up your previous assignment early and should be arriving in town this weekend," he said.

Alex Lancaster, the League's new executive director of the Mystic Bayou project. Her boss. And she didn't think she'd combed her unruly hair since driving through Arkansas.

It was possible to sigh inside her own head, right?

"They told you about the Silver Stork, didn't they?" she said, cringing slightly as she shook his hand.

"They did say it would make you easy to spot, which it did," he said brightly, gesturing towards the gathering of people who were pretending they weren't watching the exchange. "Are you hungry? We could get you fed while you're introduced to everybody."

"Oh, I would hate to intrude," she said, shaking her head. "The happy couple aren't expecting me and I couldn't just join in. It's bad manners."

"Actually, the bride is one of your prospective patients ... *and* one of your supervisors. Besides, Jillian's been on edge, waiting for you to get into town. If she knew who you were, she'd probably drag you across the square herself." He paused and shuddered. "Actually, come to think of it, I think I could be in a lot of trouble if I *didn't* introduce you. She took off Adam McTeague's eyebrows the other day when he tried to talk over a scheduled bathroom break during a committee meeting. Pregnant phoenixes are dangerous in ways I did not expect."

"Well, if you put it that way," she sighed, glancing down at her cotton shorts and jean jacket. "Should I change?"

"Jillian won't care what you're wearing. She knows you're here to help her," he said, offering her his elbow like some Austenian hero. "We're really relieved to have someone of your skill set joining us. We have Dr. Carmody running the clinic, but with predicted local population growth after the 'incident,' our mathematicians are also predicting a considerable spike in pregnancies over the next few years."

Any League employee hearing the word 'incident' could only think of one monumental event in the supernatural community over the last few months. A Louisville man named Eustace Cornwell, a satyr whose family was the basis for the Pope Lick Monster legend, lost an argument over a parking space and shifted in front of dozens of people. Most of those people had smart phones and Youtube accounts. It was simply too much exposure for the League to cover up. Humanity was informed that the nightmares that used to keep them shivering under thatched roofs at night- from fairies to sea monsters-it was all real. Real and secretly living beside them since time immemorial, and now the truth was out.

Humanity, as a whole ... did not handle this well. There was a massive wave of protests, petitions, and inaccurate Facebook posts that had some humans believing that supernatural creatures had been plotting for years to take over the world, as opposed to slowly being pushed out of all their natural spaces by the far larger human population. Watching politicians arguing on the news over whether supernaturals should have to sign up for some sort of registry, Charlotte wondered if it would have been easier if humans found out that one mythological creature existed at a time. The League could announce one a week, "Unicorns are real, but most of them are very cranky. Definitely don't try to tickle them," and then the next week, "OK, mermaids, too." She thought maybe it would have been kinder to slowly introduce the concept as opposed to ripping off the monster Band-Aid all at once.

Fortunately, the League had been preparing for this eventuality for years. They circulated millions of free copies of a book written by Jillian Ramsay, PhD, while she'd lived in Mystic Bayou, where humans and *"magique"* (the local umbrella term for all supernatural types) had lived in harmony for generations. *The Bayou: A Whole-Hearted Approach to a Blended Community* was a slightly altered version of a manual Dr. Ramsay had written for League officials, explaining how the two populations of the *"(Name Redacted) Bayou"* managed to do just that, with minimal violence, while mingling their cultures and bloodlines. Dr. Ramsay had gone on the news and talk show circuit, explaining how absolutely normal the lives of most *magique* were, that humans had likely lived next door to *magique* for years and come to no harm. So, it stood to reason that they would continue to be fine and perhaps losing their shit on a world-wide scale was a little premature.

The whole mess was unnerving, but somehow, as Alex led her through the crowd, Charlotte couldn't help but feel it was a distant problem, far from this place. The lively accordion-heavy music, bright and happy, churned over the chatter and laughter. Bottles in every conceivable color of glass hung from the tree branches overhead and she thought she saw tiny lights glowing inside of them. It was difficult to tell, in the golden afternoon light. Cheerful, home-spun floral arrangements practically dripped from every stationery surface. Small round tables placed sporadically around the square groaned under the weight of the guests' heaped plates. People were happy here, celebrating the union of two of their own–eating and drinking and dancing as if the world outside wasn't going completely bonkers. And it was a relief to feel like she was a tiny part of it.

"So how dramatic of a population increase are we talking here?" Charlotte asked.

"Well, we've had about forty 'outsiders' move here since the incident. It doesn't sound like much, but it's about forty times the normal number of people who choose to move here in an average year. Aside from League employees who have been assigned to the Bayou, that is. There are no rental properties to be had in town. Most of them are living in an 'impromptu' RV park on the end of Main Street. We have good reason to believe that's not going to slow down," Alex said.

Charlotte hummed in agreement. Since the release of Jillian's book, humans seemed to think that (Name Redacted) Bayou was a sort of supernatural Disneyland, where they could find answers for all of the universe's big questions or just live out their lifelong dream of seeing a Sasquatch. And supernatural creatures saw it as a chance to settle into the sort of life they'd always dreamed of, accepted and "normal" and living with people who understood their unique situations. Most of the changes the League made to the "public" version of the book were aimed at protecting the anonymity of the town and its residents, but … well, the internet existed. Frankly, Charlotte was surprised the town wasn't overrun.

She spotted the bridal couple, posing for a wedding party portrait in front of a carved stone fountain. The fountain featured an assortment of mythical creatures sheltered under the wings of a dragon. Jillian was wearing a long-sleeved white lace dress with an empire waist, that only served to emphasize the curve of her belly, which she was happily stroking. The bridesmaids were wearing white dresses remarkably similar to Jillian's, though their flower crowns were less ornate. The groom was a tall, lean man, hovering over Jillian with an expression that seemed equal parts joy and anxiety.

Charlotte supposed she couldn't blame him. Dr. Ramsay had a very busy couple of months recently, under intense media scrutiny. Her assurances, written and verbal, had done quite a bit to quell the public post-Pope Lick Monster panic. The headlines became less apocalyptic. The social media posts became marginally more reasonable. Markets stabilized. Charlotte had an enormous amount of respect for Jillian, particularly the icy dignity with which she testified before Congress, while very politely telling them that proposing registries to deal with the *magique* instead of, say, *having a conversation* with said *magique* was an act of self-destructive incompetence.

Like Jillian, who had also used that same glacial gravitas to inform the political types that it was "none of their business" what sort of *magie* she was, Charlotte's family had elected not to publicly announce that Charlotte and her mother, Lizzie, were a type of Romanian fae called *zana*. Not because the McBees were afraid of being hurt, but because they were afraid that Lizzie's patients and their families would decide they didn't want to be treated by a *magie*. In a location as secluded and remote as Waller Forge, Tennessee, that could be dangerous for pregnant women, human or *magie*.

Compared to a lot of modern fae she knew, Charlotte had enjoyed a relatively idyllic childhood–stable, living in one place, with both parents. Her mother was a midwife as were her ancestors, all the way down the line back to the old country before deforestation drove them across the Atlantic. Her Granny's services were so in demand in Baby Booming Appalachia, people didn't ask a lot of questions. They just wanted their babies born safe and healthy. Charlotte was fortunate that there was enough human blood in her line that she didn't have the typical fae metal allergies or the "strange spinal abnormalities." (Also known as wings.)

Lizzie McBee saw it as the family duty to provide humans with a peaceful, safe path into the world. She delighted in bestowing lifelong gifts on babies. Charlotte saw it as a heap of pressure. What if she picked the wrong gift? What if the child was meant to be a world-saving scientist and Charlotte gave her a beautiful singing voice–which was nice and all, but so was a cure for cancer. So Charlotte tried to give babies the gifts they would need in this strange, turbulent world–courage, strength, determination, and the ability to know when to abstain from social media. Let other fairies worry about temporary things like beauty and talent.

"You've stumbled into the best possible way to be introduced to all of the movers and shakers here in town," Alex told her. He pointed to the radiant blond bride. "That's obviously Jillian–author of this year's most-read book and our official liaison between locals and the League, and sometimes the rest of the world. That's her new husband, Bael Boone. He's a dragon shifter, the local sheriff, and related to half of the business-owners in town, but his family is a sore subject and you definitely don't want to bring it up. The tall guy with the beard, who looks like a biker gang and a superhero franchise had a terrifying baby, that's Mayor Zed Berend. He is very protective of … well, everybody. But the whole wedding party in particular. And he can turn into a giant bear, so it's best not to bring out that protective side. The maid of honor there, standing right next to the bride? That's Sonja Fong, the director of operations. She's the real power around here, the one who keeps us running. I just have the title. Her mate is Will Carmody, the other groomsman and our local doctor. The pretty brunette, laughing at the Mayor? Danica Teel, an energy manipulator doing research on atmospheric anomalies and the love of Zed's life."

"That is a lot to remember," she sighed, watching as the bridal party joked and jostled each other around with practiced ease.

"I have a chart with profile pictures," he whispered. "I keep it taped to the back of my closet door. I'll make you a copy, if you promise not to tell anybody. It covers every major player in town, including the mamas who will feed you into submission."

"I will memorize it and then burn it," she promised, making him chuckle.

Instead of a traditional wedding cake, the happy couple had

elected to have an enormous tower of pies arranged on a custom-made display with dozens of tiered supports. It looked mismatched and delicious, guarded by a tiny brownie whose scowling face was nearly covered by her enormous corsage. Bael and Jillian carefully fed each other a slice of some sort of chocolate pie. Charlotte noticed that no one encouraged them to smash the pie into each other's faces, which she appreciated.

In the hubbub of people claiming their pie slices, Alex called the bridal couple over. If Jillian was confused by a complete stranger showing up at her wedding reception, she didn't show it, simply smiling and kissing Charlotte's cheek when Alex introduced her.

"Sorry, I'm just flying a little high on all the nuptial joy." She giggled when Charlotte seemed surprised.

"This is Charlotte McBee, the midwife we talked about," Alex said.

If Charlotte had been surprised by the cheek kiss, she was stunned by lean, lethal-looking Bael throwing his muscled arms around her shoulders and hugging her like his life depended on it. "Oh, thank goodness!"

Dragons were possessive and dangerously protective of pregnant mates. And yet, this man was ... hugging her?

"I'm just so glad you're here," Bael said, still hugging Charlotte. "She's got a giant metal egg inside her. Please help."

Jillian shook her head, bemused. "Bael's a little overwhelmed by the idea of how the egg is going to get out."

"We'll figure that out just as soon as possible," Charlotte promised him, turning to Jillian. "You're my 'priority case,' according to Ms. Hiyashi."

"Because I'm a League employee?" Jillian asked, frowning.

"No, because we don't have any dragon-phoenix pregnancies on record ... and Ms. Hiyashi really likes you," Charlotte said. "She knows how hard you've been working and wants to make sure you're taken care of."

"Aw, I'm still getting used to the idea that she knows my name," Jillian sighed, her eyes getting misty.

Charlotte chuckled. "Well, obviously, you're pretty busy right now, but how soon would you like to have an exam? I'm assuming you're having a honeymoon of some sort?"

Jillian sniffed and waved her hand in front of her eyes to ward off the oncoming tears. "Yes, I won't be able to help you acclimate to your new job as I will be on a brief honeymoon, in a cabin in the middle of nowhere, that Bael will not give anyone coordinates for, in fear that people will track us down and tell us all about their problems."

"It tends to happen a lot," Bael muttered, having finally let go of Charlotte.

Jillian added, "Followed by being sequestered until I give birth."

"Well, I'll be with you the whole time, so at least you won't be lonely! This is my cell phone number. If you have problems at all, you call me. Doesn't matter how minor you think it is, or how silly you feel, you call me."

Jillian wrapped her arms around Charlotte's shoulders. "Thank you. You seem nice, I almost hate to tell you that the 'confinement' will be in a cave in the middle of nowhere, also in a place Bael will not provide coordinates for.

Charlotte snickered. "I once helped a Yeti give birth inside a glacier. I can handle it."

"In the meantime, Dr. Carmody will be able to answer all of your questions and help you figure out a patient list," Jillian said. "To be honest, we don't know how long we're going to need you. With all the people coupling up lately, it would seem like it could be a while. The baby betting pool on Sonja vs. Dani has been vicious."

"That offends a lot of my sensibilities," Sonja muttered.

"Noted, but I can't do anything about it," Jillian told her.

Before Charlotte could respond, there was a commotion by

the pie stand. A tall man with coltishly long limbs tripped, almost falling face-first into the tower of pastries. Suddenly, the burly mayor, Zed, was behind him, catching him by the elbows, stopping his momentum so effectively that he only bumped the stand a little bit. Sonja ran over and steadied the tower and adjusted the few pies that had been jostled, back into place.

As Zed set the man back on his feet, Charlotte felt a zing of awareness up her spine. Somewhere nearby, the consequences of fairy magic were rippling over the air.

Zed curved an enormous hand around the poor man's shoulder. "Leonard, buddy, I like you, but don't endanger the pie."

Leonard sighed, "Thanks, man."

Charlotte took a closer look at "Leonard." At first glance, the man didn't have the magnetic pull of smoldering Zed or elegant Bael, but he had a kind face. Warm brown eyes and sandy hair, square jaw, a narrow, well-formed nose, and a sensitive mouth. But there was something ... off about him. He radiated a chaotic energy that was mismatched with his body. She paused, watching him. Was this poor man cursed?

Charlotte made a mental note to ask about this later. Today was not a day for fairy business. It was for making good impressions and getting some of that pie.

"Poor Leonard," Jillian sighed. "I told him not to get so wound up about making sure the buffet was timed right. People don't starve here in Mystic Bayou. The mamas wouldn't allow it."

Alex patted Charlotte's arm. "Speaking of which, I'm sure you're hungry after all that time on the road, Charlotte. How about I get you a plate?"

"Oh, I couldn't." Charlotte's brows lifted. Was this how her boss treated all new hires? Fetching them pie? If they put that sort of thing on the brochure, there would be no recruitment problems at the League. If the League did recruitment brochures, which they did not.

"You spend a lot of time telling me what you 'couldn't' do. I hope that's not a sign of what us working together will be like," Alex said, winking at her. "It's nonsense. You've been driving all day. I don't mind. Any allergies I should know about?"

"Pushy supervisors?" she suggested.

"I'm giving you the *spicy* gumbo, just for that," he told her, turning towards a long table set with what looked like hundreds of dishes.

"Welcome to the Bayou!" a voice boomed to Charlotte's left, making her jump. She turned to find Zed standing behind her, offering her a plate of some strange chocolate and fruit concoction. The thick chocolate filling oozed with pink chunks of … celery?

"That there is chocolate rhubarb pie, a local specialty," Zed informed her, smiling broadly.

"Oh, thanks, uh, Mr. Mayor, you didn't have to do that," Charlotte said.

"Sure I did," Zed replied. "You're here to take care of our Jillian and who knows who else. We've got a Bayou baby boom coming down the tracks at us. We want to make sure you feel at home."

When Charlotte paused, mid-reach for the plate, and sent him a curious look, Zed added, "Bear hearing is better than people think. Siobhan's a little busy to help you pick your pie, but I figured most people like chocolate."

"Do I look so tired that I can't pick my own pie?" Charlotte asked.

Jillian laughed. "Siobhan is a brownie and she has this strange ability not only to make amazing pies, but to choose the best pie to meet your spiritual and emotional needs. It's a thing here. And believe it or not, you won't be disappointed. Her chocolate rhubarb is magical, either way. You can't lose."

"*Any* pie would meet my spiritual and emotional needs right now," Charlotte sighed, shoveling a bite into her mouth. She put down her fork and leveled a very serious look at Jillian. "I need to find Siobhan and give her all of my money."

"That's how most people respond," Jillian said, patting her arm.

Alex hadn't been kidding about the number of mamas who would press food on her. Before she could sit down with the enormous platter of shrimp, rice dressing, crawfish bread, boudin, cornbread, and weirdly enough, *spatzel*, a half-dozen or so mothers sailed by to pile more food on her plate.

"They're scoping you out as a potential mate for their sons," Sonja informed her, placing an ice-cold beer bottle by Charlotte's plate and settling into the chair next to her.

Charlotte wasn't sure whether her sudden paralysis was from being star-struck by so many League luminaries sitting at the table with her or from the announcement that she was about to be aggressively match-made. She'd been through this before, her trailer door getting knocked on constantly as her little mini-fridge filled with not-entirely-edible casseroles. Convincing the masses of interfering parents–most of them trying to launch their adult sons out of their houses–that she did not, in fact, want to take said sons off of their hands, had a tendency to interfere with her job.

Apparently sensing her distress, Sonja added, "It's nothing personal, it happens every time a newcomer moves into town. So far, all of the League transplants have found partners here and settled down. The mamas see it as a way to secure their kids' lives here in town, *and* a couple of grandkids."

Charlotte pressed her lips together and tried to find the most diplomatic way of saying, "Please, no."

"They've probably stocked your fridge already," Zed told her. "I don't think I've ever seen my *maman* without Tupperware in her car."

"But the trailer is locked," Charlotte objected.

Zed grinned at her. "It's cute that you think locks will keep them out."

Charlotte shook her head. "I don't like that."

"Can't say I blame you," Sonja assured her. "The social rules down here are a little different. Jillian and Bael had to post the invitation on the community billboard, because you exclude one person and there will be a reckoning, either magically or socially. If we hadn't put Clarissa in charge of the food, I don't know if we would have had any idea what to do. But despite my catering ineptitude, if you have any questions about anyone or anything, I am your point person. Because if Will doesn't know, I'll know."

"Meanwhile, I'll be in a cave somewhere," Jillian muttered.

Sonja grinned at her and wrapped her arm around her shoulders. "Bael wants you to have a chance to rest, sweetie. Not to mention some post-wedding privacy. Take advantage. Trust me and Leonard to keep things running while you're gone. You'll be back bossing us around in no time."

"It's not that I don't trust you. It's that I don't like missing out on things," Jillian replied, her pout making Sonja laugh. "It takes weeks for me to catch up!"

At the mention of the pie-endangerer, Charlotte scanned the crowd for Leonard. Something about that skittering sensation of fairy magic up her spine in the middle of a wedding reception made her incredibly uneasy. She looked for him among the smiling, laughing faces celebrating a couple so clearly on their way to a bright and happy future.

But he was gone.

2

LEONARD

*W*hen you nearly take out your boss's de facto wedding cake because of a fairy curse, surely your next day at work had to be easier by comparison. Right?

Leonard O'Donnell had been prepared for *something* to happen at Jillian's wedding. Even though he had no direct role in the ceremony, being around that many people, in dress clothes, with the emotional stakes so high, he knew the jitters would get the best of him and disaster would follow. He hadn't expected to trip and come dangerously close to toppling Siobhan's masterwork of pie, but with the curse, you never really knew what was going to happen on big occasions for O'Donnells. His poor cousin, Shannon, had dropped her groom's wedding ring during the ceremony, then knocked a candelabra over when she bent to pick it up and set her gown on fire. If not for a quick-thinking flower girl who doused her in holy water, Shannon would have spent her honeymoon in the ER.

The O'Donnell curse was no laughing matter–a whole family of people who got more clumsy as they got more nervous. Fortunately, Zed had caught Leonard before he did too much damage to the pies. He adored Jillian, who had been accepting and understanding of his "condition" from the moment he was hired as her executive assistant. Knowing that he could potentially do much worse before the bouquet toss, he'd given the bride his best wishes and gotten the hell out of dodge. It was what was best for everybody.

But then Monday morning, he walked into the administrative building to find that Jessica Galanis tried to pull a power move the minute Jillian was officially on her honeymoon, by moving Leonard's desk to the "annex."

Despite the fact that *la faille*–a mystical rip in the fabric of the universe that had, until recently, threatened to unravel and unleash its body-altering energy into Southern Louisiana and beyond– had closed, Mystic Bayou still offered a wealth of research opportunities in areas like genetics, meteorology, and economics for the League. Rather than closing up shop, the League was expanding its interest in the Bayou with a permanent administrative building/research center. Unfortunately, construction on that center wouldn't begin until late spring.

The annex was technically a temporary extension of the administrative trailer, tacked on to give Sonja and Jillian room to work after Alex had taken over Jillian's position. Alex was smart enough not to move Jillian too far away from Sonja–not just because they'd been close friends for years, but because together, they made minor miracles happen.

The same awareness could not be contributed to Jessica, Leonard's nemesis. He knew it wasn't normal for an executive assistant to have an archenemy. His job centered on managing Sonja and Jillian's schedules and workload. Jessica was Alex's assistant, and was supposed to be focused on him. Unlike nearly every other job in the Bayou, their positions were not fraught with peril. And yet, Jessica fought for domination of that trailer like it was her own personal kingdom and he was a usurper. She didn't like that his was the first face people saw when they walked in, while she was seated closer to Alex's door, facing the wall. She didn't like that *he* was considered the gatekeeper to not only Sonja and Jillian, but Alex as well. She didn't like that she'd gone to a university to study how to best optimize an executive's workflow and schedule, while Leonard had just fallen into the job.

Leonard thought that maybe they could have bonded, both being cursed because of the actions of an ancient ancestor, but no. Jessica seemed to think that being a direct descendant of King Midas made her some sort of *magique* elite. Literally everything she touched turned to gold. She'd actually helped the League out a few times when they'd foreseen budget shortfalls, turning a few old vehicles to gold so they could be melted down into capital for the League.

By comparison, Leonard was just an oaf who bumped into things.

His only comfort was that the curse prevented Jessica from enjoying the fruits of her abilities–which he supposed was the definition of a curse. The stories about Midas emphasized his inability to eat or drink, but they didn't mention anything about the gold disappearing from Midas' hands when he tried to spend it. Jessica could help other people (or secret government agencies), but if she tried to hand her gold to someone in exchange for goods or services, it would fade into nothing. Her family had sent banks all over the world into a state of panic over the years, depositing huge piles of gold bricks, only for the vaults to be empty the next day and their accounts returned to their previous balance. Apparently, it was meant to teach Midas and his bloodline about selfishness and helping others. Magic could be a real pain in the ass sometimes.

Jessica was certainly imperious as Leonard spun around in the lobby like a doofus, trying to figure out where his desk had moved over the weekend. Any evidence that he'd ever worked there had disappeared, and was replaced with Jessica's strange round "work module" based on some Swedish principle of open workflow and clutter destruction.

She settled her long-legged frame in her module, swishing her long sable-colored ponytail over the shoulder of her designer jacket. She dressed to impress, but somehow lacked the elegance that Sonja managed to exude so easily.

"Don't bother getting comfortable," she'd told him, shooting the cuffs of the prim white leather driving gloves she wore to keep her hands from "goldening" everything she touched. "I took the liberty of having your desk moved to the annex. It just makes more sense, as Jillian's duties become more ... limited."

"I'm sure this has nothing to do with the fact that Jillian's out of the office," he deadpanned.

"I don't know what you mean," she said, smiling blithely as she entered her password into her computer.

"What's next, you're going to try to call a meeting of department heads without Jillian? Try to stage a one-woman coup over the coffee supplies?" Leonard asked.

"If you have a problem with the way I organize the office, you can always complain to the head administrator," Jessica replied.

"*You're* the head administrator," Leonard said.

Jessica's lips curled into a smirk. "Yes, I know."

Sonja walked into the office, three binders stacked in her arms. Her sleek brow lifted at the appearance of secretarial turmoil "What is happening here?"

All appearances of smirking on Jessica's face made way for an expression of sweetness and light. "Oh, just a little re-organization, streamlining operations, moving the fluff out of the way."

Sonja, who had been (a much better) head administrator before being promoted to director of operations, frowned. "Jessica, I believe we had a conversation where we discussed not referring to our colleagues as 'fluff.'"

Jessica's shrug was more of a wiggle of the shoulders, as if insulting Leonard wasn't worth the full gesture. "Well, Sonja, change is necessary as we enter this new era for the Mystic Bayou facility. And we both know how difficult it is for people to accept change. Sometimes, you just have to guide them through it."

Leonard did not appreciate being talked about like he wasn't present ... or smart enough to understand the conversation.

"I'm just trying to maximize the potential of the space while reducing confusion about our roles," Jessica said

Sonja smiled patiently. "Jessica, you know I appreciate proactivity, but you don't have the authority to make those decisions. The system that we've had in place for weeks works quite well, thank you. Please, put the desk back where it was."

"But Mr. Lancaster gave me the—"

"I will discuss this with Mr. Lancaster. Put it back, please." Sonja's smile was just as cool as Jessica's, though there was underlying bite to her voice as she added, "*Now.* Leonard, if you could join me in my office?"

He tried not to sneer at Jessica as he followed Sonja into her office. He really did. She sighed as she rounded the ever-growing display of plants that bloomed around her desk. Leonard flopped into the "guest" chair. "Thanks, Sonja."

"Think nothing of it," she said, waving his gratitude away as if knocking the wind out of the office bully's sails was nothing. "Some people become administrators because they enjoy controlling small worlds in a universe that is pure chaos." Sonja laid a slim, elegant hand against her delicate peach silk blouse.

"Other people become administrators because they like pushing people around," she added. "I haven't decided which Jessica is, but I hope she's just trying to justify why her position is vital to the organization. I'm trying to be patient with her, but no matter what, I've got your back, Len. You were here first and you are far less annoying."

"Thanks, Sonja." Leonard pulled his phone out and they spent a few minutes reviewing her schedule, unanswered emails, and the duties they would be expected to cover during Jillian's honeymoon and maternity leave. Leonard's position would be more forward-facing, as he would be recording locals' concerns.

Honestly, Leonard was sort of looking forward to it. He'd liked the vast majority of the Mystic Bayou residents he'd met. They were strange and fascinating people with even weirder backgrounds than his own. It was the only place he'd ever lived where he could be honest about his life and be completely accepted. All he had to say was "fairy curse" and people just nodded and moved along with their business.

"I know it's going to be demanding for you, but I'm confident you can handle it," Sonja told him. "Now, if you'll join me at the clinic, we have a new midwife to initiate into the ways of Mystic Bayou."

"Jillian's midwife is here!" Leonard exclaimed. For weeks, Jillian had been talking about the specialist with extensive experience in rare hybrid pregnancies, as if this Charlotte woman was a golden lifeline. "How did I miss that?"

"She got here right before the pie stand thing," Sonja said gently.

"Well, hell," he sighed. "But it's just the normal new employee, 'please don't do anything evil' meet-and-greet, right? Do you really need me for that?"

"Not really, but it means Jessica will have to figure out how to move your desk on her own," Sonja said.

"That sounds just fair enough to be properly vengeful," he said, standing and gesturing grandly towards the door. "Lead the way!"

Jessica was still trying to get maintenance workers to come help her move Leonard's enormous work station back as they left. Leonard figured that was justice.

There weren't a lot of advantages of living in a place as small as Mystic Bayou. There were no chain stores or Starbucks or even a bar. But he could walk basically anywhere in town from his office door. Or his trailer door, which happened to be about three hundred feet from his office door. He hadn't bought gas since he moved to town. They walked across the street to the clinic, past the giant silver airstream that had sort of appeared during the wedding reception. The side featured a highly-stylized white bird over swooping lettering that read, "The Silver Stork."

That was different.

The clinic was technically an old veterinary hospital that Sonja had almost single-handedly converted to treat people so the town could have a doctor again. And that doctor happened to be Will Carmody, a Mystic Bayou-born physician who happened to be Sonja's boyfriend. And he happened to be a mermaid, sort of. Leonard wasn't sure how that worked but honestly, he was afraid to ask.

"Will? Love of my life!" Sonja called, walking through the brightly painted waiting room. "I'm here! With Leonard!"

Will's ridiculously handsome face appeared in his office door, a brilliantly white smile blooming at the sight of Sonja. Living in the Bayou could really wear on the old self-esteem when you were just a regular-looking guy. Not to mention those magazine perfect-looking guys could also turn into dragons and tigers and honest-to-God bears. But Will was a nice guy, and he made Sonja happy—and he'd thought to include Leonard in a couple of "dude gatherings" with Bael and Zed, which was pretty cool of him.

"Hey there, sweetheart," Will purred, kissing her in what could be considered a professional manner. "Just in time. I made coffee."

"That's why you're my favorite," she told him, as Will waved them into the office.

"I was just reviewing some cases for Charlotte," Will said.

As he was walking through the door, Leonard dropped the binders he was holding. He was stepping forward as he did this and his foot connected, kicking the binders across the floor and under Will's desk. Because, of course, he did.

"Charlotte" was the most beautiful thing he'd ever seen.

Huge, thickly lashed eyes the color of the summer sky seemed to dominate a delicate heart-shaped face. Her lush mouth was painted a blushing pink he would happily spend hours contemplating if she wouldn't find that sort of thing creepy. Her thick dark curls were pulled back from her face in a neat twist at the crown of her head, a complement to the crisp blue scrubs she wore. And she was so small. He'd never seen someone so proportionately petite outside of the Tinkerbell cartoons his nieces loved. How was it possible to fit so *much* into one tiny package?

"No, don't call women 'things,'" his brain chided him. *"You know better than that."* But all other cognitive functions were just gone. His brain had abandoned him. Blood rushed to his cheeks and he felt the familiar rush of anxiety that was almost always followed by disaster and broken glass and once, the destruction of a life-size fiberglass blue whale at a natural history museum.

He focused on the breathing exercise his mother had taught him, focusing his rampant thoughts and slowing his heartrate. He thought of the forest near his parents' weekend cabin, deep and green and shadowed. He thought of the music of the river behind the cabin, the water dancing over the moss-covered rocks. The forest had been his happy place as a child, unlike the classmates who had been warned *never* to wander out of their sterile, safe suburb. The more he calmed his nerves, the less the curse would affect him. And the fewer whale replicas would suffer.

Will eyed Leonard, but having reviewed Leonard's case extensively, said nothing beyond, "I'll get those."

Leonard cleared his throat. "Uh, hi," he said, walking across the room like it was a damn tightrope, just so he could shake her hand. "Leonard O'Donnell. Nice to meet you."

"Charlotte McBee." A strange spark, like blue lightning, crackled between their hands. Charlotte yelped, her eyes going ever wider as she shook off the shock. She giggled, a bell-like noise that did strange things to Leonard's pulse. Somehow, his cheeks grew hotter and he backed away, sitting in his chair before he could do anymore harm.

"Sorry about that," he muttered.

She smiled sweetly and he felt his heart break just a little in its warmth. "No problem. Static electricity."

Leonard made a noise that was somehow both squeaky and grumbling. Could he belly crawl out of the room? It seemed like the option least likely to result in injury to others or further embarrassment to himself.

"So, I know we probably overwhelmed you a little bit at the wedding. We're just so happy you're here." Sonja handed Charlotte a bright blue *Welcome to League Employment in the Mystic Bayou Office* binder and a League copy of Jillian's book. "This is a brief overview of Bayou-specific policies, and just in case you haven't read it, Jillian's history of the Bayou, *la faille* and the League's involvement here."

Charlotte nodded, recently having learned about *la faille*—the interdimensional rift located in the swamp—that was responsible for Mystic Bayou's supernatural population. Over the years it had either drawn shifters and fae to Mystic Bayou or changed human residents at a genetic level, turning them into *magique*. According to the League officials who requested her presence here, the rift had recently been closed, but before that had happened, it had been a beacon for supernatural creatures of all kinds.

Charlotte looked at the book and nodded.

"We know it's a lot," continued Sonja. "Especially with everything else you're doing, so just go at your own pace. There won't be a test, I promise."

"Thanks," Charlotte said, her grin not reflecting any intimidation.

"So how did you get into magical pregnancies?" Leonard blurted suddenly, making Sonja and Will stare. "As a profession?"

Oh, come on, was this an exciting new feature of his curse? *Verbal* clumsiness? Had he and the replicated sea life not suffered enough?

"I just sort of fell into it," she said, her southern accent somehow more lyrically musical than the Cajun voices he'd become accustomed to since moving to Louisiana. "I mean, I was already interested in midwifery. It's sort of the family business, going back to my several times-great-granny. She was one of those mountain women who cured what ailed you with a combination of real medicine, magic, and just enough power of suggestion to keep everybody in line. And then, after my studies, I worked in a clinic where I just happened to have a patient who was a badger shifter married to a *chupacabra*."

Will shuddered. "Wow."

"It took me a shameful amount of time to figure out I was dealing with two shapeshifters, and how different that makes a pregnancy. Every shifter's gestation period is different. Their symptoms and cravings and complications, they're all unique. Anyway, once I put the context clues together, I was able to meet with them privately, let them know I was aware of their special genetic circumstances and I would do everything I could to bring their baby safely into the world while protecting their secret. They were such a sweet couple. The daddy painted my trailer as a thank you," Charlotte said.

"They were so happy with me that they contacted their local League office to tell them, assuming that the League appointed me to handle shifter pregnancies. The League liked what they heard and hired me as a freelancer. The more I worked, the more I learned. The more I learned, the more my skills were in demand. And now I'm here."

"I'm so glad you're here," Leonard breathed.

Across the room, Will covered his snicker with a cough. "Sorry, man."

"Selkie humor," Sonja assured Charlotte, while giving Will an arch look.

Will sobered quickly. "Which was her none too subtle way of telling you I'm a selkie, a seal shapeshifter. Other than increased strength and speed, it's really not an issue unless I'm near water. And even then, I'll just outswim you."

"He's exaggerating," Sonja insisted. "He can also hold his breath for a very long time."

Will snorted.

"So, everybody just talks about their supernatural status in the open here?" Charlotte asked. "I've never worked in an environment like that, not even working with League clinics."

"It is considered rude by the locals, to directly ask about *magie* status, but not to bring it up yourself. I, for instance, am human," Sonja said.

"But with added awesomeness," Will insisted while Sonja preened graciously. "It would just be unfair to everybody else to give you superpowers."

Charlotte looked to Leonard, who just couldn't seem to produce the words, *I'm a human whose family has lived under a fairy curse for hundreds of years.* It was the first time he'd had any trouble saying so while living there.

When he didn't respond, she simply said, "I'm a *zana*, it's sort of a broad term, catch-all for Romanian fae folk. My particular branch of the 'family' were forest dwellers in the classic 'fairy godmother' vein. They blessed unborn babies, helped lost children get out of the woods, rewarded decent people for their virtues, that sort of thing. Their affection for unborn humans eventually led to midwifery. My several-times-great-grandmother saw the writing on the wall, in terms of the old world versus new, and how people were intruding on the forest. She adopted a common last name, learned human ways, and made her way to America in the 1830s. Somehow, she ended up in Tennessee. It seemed a better long-term plan than cursing an entire population of woodcutters."

She smiled warmly at Leonard, as if prompting him–again–to take his turn. But his mouth had turned dry, staring at her lovely little face. He swallowed heavily. It wasn't so much her fae nature, but the casual way she'd talked of throwing curses around made him nervous.

Charlotte was an unknown quantity and Leonard's reaction to that made him feel like a grade-A jackass. Her being born with special abilities was no more her fault than being born with a curse was his fault. Her being beautiful and interesting and kind had his hormones in over-drive, which was the real complication in the situation. He was practically tied in knots, he was so nervous. And that was never a good thing.

He couldn't move, which was probably for the best, because he would probably trip if he tried to get up and fall out of the first-story window to his death. And even if he managed to make it out of the room unscathed, he didn't want to hurt this woman's feelings because of his own irrational issues. So he sat there quietly, mulling over the possibility of time travel, so he could go back to visit the O'Donnell ancestor that started this mess and kick his ass.

Sonja apparently picked up on Leonard's inward meltdown because she quickly moved the agenda along to the next department head meeting. They chatted about the various departments and how Charlotte might need to interact with them. She was warned about Adam McTeague and his tendency to dominate meetings with his overblown opinions regarding his own economics research. Leonard didn't contribute much to the conversation, and was grateful to Sonja and Will for making up for his silence.

As the conversation wound down, Sonja handed Charlotte a manila envelope. "Now comes the thing that the League likes best."

"Paperwork?" Charlotte guessed.

"So many forms," Sonja told her in an almost apologetic fashion. "Most of them are very specific non-disclosure agreements. Don't feel like you have to get them all back to me today. Just finish them when you have time. And with that, Leonard and I will be on our way. You two go make Mystic Bayou a healthier place."

Will grinned at her and gave her a smacking kiss.

"Nice to meet you," Leonard told Charlotte, before moving toward the door with near-surgical concentration. She smiled and waved, probably trying to avoid another static shock. He turned to wave back and somehow, that motion threw him off balance and he tipped forward, nearly face-planting against the door frame. Sonja caught his arm before his nose made contact with the metal.

"Are you all right?" Charlotte cried, coming closer to cup his jaw in her hands, inspecting his face for damage. That same crackling energy rippled up the side of his face, making him shudder in dread and delight.

"I'm fine," he muttered, stepping away from her. "Happens all the time."

He walked out of the clinic as fast as he dared. Sonja only caught up with him half-way across the street. Everything would be fine. He just had to avoid beautiful, compelling Charlotte McBee and he would be fine. Or at least, he wouldn't be injured in some humiliating fashion, possibly involving dragon fire or giant porcupine quills.

"You OK?" Sonja asked as they walked back to the admin building.

"Sure. I just hope that Jessica hasn't moved my desk into the swamp by the time we get back," Leonard said.

3

CHARLOTTE

*W*henever her mother got stressed, Lizzie McBee would say that she was "blessed with work." Well, Charlotte had blessings coming out of her ears.

Still, working kept her mind off of the thousands of moving in tasks she needed to do. And then there was the strange riddle of Leonard O'Donnell. Charlotte saw him freeze up and shut down every time she approached him. Even if he was engaged in conversation, relaxed and laughing, he would just go quiet and still. He moved so rigidly, she was afraid his bones would crack.

Some people just felt uneasy around the fae. It was easy to understand, she supposed. Fae could be petty creatures, seeking disproportionate vengeance for relatively small slights. The Grimms' original fairy tales were practically subtitled, "Long and detailed cautionary stories about pissing off the fae." She tried not to let it hurt her feelings, but well, it stung.

And because her romantic nature was decidedly perverse, of course, she found Leonard incredibly attractive. Normally, she was a bit intimidated by men who were so much taller than her. But Leonard had the kindest eyes, with all the warmth and sweetness of melted chocolate. She found herself wondering what it would feel like to have those long, lean arms wrapped around her. In the middle of her workdays, she would picture his large hands spanning across her back. And then she would start thinking about height-anatomical proportionality and–

No, no. She wouldn't date a man who didn't like her. She'd tried that. It didn't work. Well, honestly, she didn't date much, but somehow, she always managed to choose men who were decidedly unavailable emotionally. It wasn't all that bad in the long run. She was an admitted workaholic, and her schedule was often filled with surprises and emergencies. She didn't have the time for someone looking for long-term commitment.

Deep down, she wanted what her parents had, but she just hadn't found someone she thought she could tolerate forever and ever. Hank and Lizzie McBee had fallen in love at first sight–or at least, "intense like." At twenty, Hank had taken one look at Lizzie and knew that she was it for him. Lizzie had been a little harder to convince, unsure of how perfectly human Hank McBee would respond to her fae nature. (The answer was "enthusiastically.") They'd gotten married as soon as Lizzie's mother would allow it, after she finished her midwife training. And they never regretted settling down so young. They didn't see the point in dating other people when they found what they wanted on the first try.

So maybe subconsciously, Charlotte picked men she could hold at a distance without regret. Somehow, she didn't think she could do that with Leonard O'Donnell. So she distracted herself with patients. Jillian was coming in for an exam that morning. Analah Agarwal was expecting her exceedingly healthy tiger-slash-lion shifter baby any day now. Fortunately, it didn't involve complex magics fighting it out with each other, just a lot of muscle and teeth. And she was sure Dani Teel was pregnant, but didn't realize it yet.

Charlotte had come home from the grocery the day before to find Zed and Dani standing outside of the Silver Stork.

"Hi, Charlotte," he said, sheepishly taking her groceries out of her hands. "We, uh, weren't trying to look in your windows or anything."

"He didn't mean for that to sound so creepy. He's way more interested in the engineering of the trailer than your underwear," Dani promised her, rubbing absently at her sternum, as if she was suffering heartburn. Charlotte's head tilted, listening to the tiny pattering sound only she could hear from Dani's middle. Between that and the lovely, warm energy she could feel radiating from the energy witch, Charlotte could barely contain her giggle.

This town was going to be so much fun.

"Would you like to take a look inside?" Charlotte asked.

Zed gave a nod more suited to a small child than a public figure the size of a boulder. She handed him the keys. "Go ahead."

"I'll just put these grocery bags on the counter!" he said, fiddling the keys into the lock. Once inside, he yelled. "It's so girly inside! And everything smells so nice!"

"We live in a man-made cave. It doesn't take much to impress him," Dani sighed, turning to Charlotte. "You sure you don't mind a stranger just going into your space like that?"

Charlotte shrugged. "Eh, the Silver Stork has served as an exam room and once, a birthing suite for a very tense manticore, so it's not exactly sacred personal space. I just keep the unmentionable stuff locked up."

"Considering the number of people who will be dropping by that's a good idea." Dani stopped suddenly, turning a sickly shade of green. "Excuse me."

Dani turned precisely ninety degrees away from Charlotte and vomited all over the blacktop. Charlotte poked her head inside the trailer and pulled a can of ginger ale she always kept on hand for her patients. Zed was engrossed in the overhead storage compartments but when he heard retching noises outside, he moved towards the door—or at least, he tried to, Charlotte was standing in the way.

"*Abeille?* You all right?" he called, when he couldn't fit around Charlotte in the narrow corridor.

"You might give her a minute," Charlotte whispered. "Nobody wants to be seen all vomit-y by the man they love."

"You sure?" he frowned, craning his neck towards the windows.

She nodded and took the soda outside, pressing it into Dani's hand. "Do you feel better now?"

Dani nodded, her dark curls bouncing as she wiped at her mouth. "I'm sure it's nothing, food poisoning, maybe. I haven't felt right this morning since my breakfast pie." And then she turned ghost-white and said, "Please never tell Siobhan I said that. If she thinks I'm blaming her for throwing up, she'll never let me near the pie again."

"My lips are sealed," Charlotte promised.

It was tempting, to start asking questions, to lead Dani to her own conclusions about her condition. But Charlotte didn't want to ruin the surprise for her. She figured she had about two weeks before Dani came in for an exam. Later, as she organized her equipment in the clinic's designated prenatal room, Charlotte decided she would shelve all thoughts of Dani's treatment plans in the same place where she stored the muddlesome puzzle of Leonard O'Donnell.

Will had set her up in the largest exam room, not just to make the expecting mothers more comfortable, but because there was always the possibility of patients shifting into large-scale animals while freaking out during an exam. Still, Charlotte wasn't sure there was enough room for a full-size dragon, and she was one hundred percent sure she didn't want to find out. She was excited and yet, a little terrified, as she gave the exam room one last cleaning.

"The newlyweds!" she exclaimed as Jillian knocked on the doorframe.

"Good morning." Jillian looked flushed and happy, exactly how you'd expect a bride to look post-honeymoon, just a little more pregnant. And Bael was every inch the doting new husband and expectant father. What Charlotte didn't expect was for Zed to follow them into the exam room, shutting the door behind him.

Charlotte lifted her dark brow. "Mayor Berend, um, did you have some questions for me? This appointment is really just for Jillian and her birthing partner."

"Technically, I'm here in my mayoral capacity. It's not good for the citizens for a panicky dragon father to be rampaging through the Bayou. Also, I'm the one who will be getting you out to the birthing site, so Jillian thought it would be a good idea for me to sit in," Zed said.

Charlotte looked to Jillian for confirmation, only to receive a brilliant grin. The midwife shrugged. "You're in charge here, Dr. Ramsay."

"Any instructions for me?" Bael asked, swallowing heavily as he eyed the ultrasound machine.

"Try to relax," Charlotte replied. "The more comfortable you are with me now, the better off we'll be when you're in dragon form. I do not look good surrounded by reptilian flames."

"It's not that bad," Zed assured her. Jillian shot the mayor an incredulous look and Zed added, "Well, I don't want to scare her!"

Charlotte went about the business of her normal patient intake. Bael and Zed had to duck out at several points to give Jillian privacy, but they handled it with good humor. Jillian was in remarkably good health for someone who worked as hard as she did, in a high-stress position. Of course, Jillian also vomited blue lava on occasion, so Charlotte supposed everything balanced out in the end.

Almost self-consciously, Charlotte laid a hand on an old leather-bound journal on the counter. While she'd rejected the magic books, Lizzie had loaned Charlotte her ancestor's diaries for her travels. Granny Una had dealt with all sorts of supernatural pregnancies when she moved to the New World. Like had a way of recognizing like back then, and all *magique* mothers knew Una Popescu's kitchen was a safe haven for all pregnant females, no matter what the species. Una kept careful records of her patients, the strange quirks and perils of their pregnancies and how she'd handled them. It had provided an invaluable guide to the women in Charlotte's family.

"So, I'll be honest, I've delivered dragon babies and I've delivered phoenix babies, but I've never delivered a hybrid of the two," she told them. "And I have never delivered a giant metal egg for a non-dragon before. But no one else has, either, to my knowledge. I'm approaching this in the same way I imagine you approached your wedding. We'll take a mix of cues from both of your biologies to make you as comfortable as possible. Anything you don't want, as long as it doesn't create an unsafe situation, we'll do away with it. So, to start, I'm assuming you want the birth to take place in your cave in phoenix form?"

"Well, I definitely don't want to try to push a giant metal egg out of my human parts," Jillian retorted, making both Zed and Bael cross their legs in their seats.

"Agreed. Now, in terms of safety," Charlotte said. "The last phoenix shifter I attended laid her egg in a nest of smoldering coals. And she burst into flames during contractions. So, I will be wearing fireproof gear for my own protection."

"Smart," Zed said. "I think we have firefighter gear in the parish hall. You could borrow it."

"Thanks. That's very helpful. Now, let's take a look at the baby!" Charlotte said, wheeling the ultrasound cart towards the exam table.

"Do I get to stay for the ultrasound?" Zed whispered, his eyes going wide. "Is that all right, *bebelle?*"

"Well, someone has to catch Bael if he passes out. He got a little misty last time." Jillian laughed and squeezed Zed's hand as Charlotte drizzled warmed gel on her stomach. Charlotte turned toward the wall to hide her grin. Zed was going to be downright adorable with his own partner's pregnancy.

"I didn't cry," Bael sniffed. "I had something in my eye."

"Tears, probably," Zed said, smirking.

"You want to talk about Herr Scalesenstuff and Dr. Squeakenstein?" Bael asked.

"No," Zed muttered quietly as Charlotte switched on the ultrasound machine.

Technically, Charlotte wasn't a qualified ultrasound tech, but she'd had to learn how to use the equipment herself to protect her patients' privacy. It wasn't like you could go to a regular human prenatal clinic when the scan could show your baby had wings.

The room fell silent as the screen lit, showing a black-and-white crescent with a big dark oval in the center. Charlotte lifted a brow and pressed the button to listen to the baby's heartbeat. It sounded like a faint gonging sound, a tiny heart thrumming against the metal shell that contained it.

Charlotte pressed her lips together, nodding. "So, that's a big metal egg."

"I have concerns," Jillian said, nodding.

"I thought you were exaggerating," Zed marveled. "It really is a big metal egg."

"I told you, I wasn't being obstinate about a gender reveal party. The baby won't let us get a look at him or her," Bael told Zed.

Zed snickered. "The mystery is driving my *maman* crazy. She's bought so much green yarn, she's about to crowd Mel out of the house. Not that I mind, you know, if Mel has to move out."

"You need to accept that your mother is an adult with a sex life," Jillian told Zed as he literally recoiled across the room. "Kind of a vigorous sex life, if Bonita De Los Santos and her famous gossip is to be believed."

"*Le diable!*" Zed gasped. "We agreed never to speak it, Jillian! Never!"

"Jillian, we talked about this," Bael told her, even as he smirked. "Referring to geriatric sexual practices is funny, but not in front of Zed."

"Mel is my honorary father figure and Zed's sort of stepfather," Jillian explained to Charlotte. "He's living with Zed's mom."

Bael muttered, "Relationships can get very complicated in the Bayou."

"Well, perplexing family trees aside, you're doing everything you should, pregnancy-wise. I think we're looking at the next two weeks or so. Pay attention to your body and what it's telling you. Work as long as you're comfortable," Charlotte said.

"Ha!" Jillian shot a triumphant look at Bael, who frowned.

And then Charlotte added, "As long as you get a sensible amount of rest and fluids and don't overdo it."

"Ha!" Bael retorted. "And just so we're clear, Miss Charlotte, who determines what is a reasonable amount of rest, fluids, and overdoing it?"

Charlotte's lips drew back in a frown. "An impartial third party?"

Both Jillian and Bael looked to Zed, who mused, "Probably Sonja. She's the most adult out of all of us."

"And she's the only one Jillian will listen to," Bael added, nodding.

"Me and the giant metal egg are right here," Jillian noted, pointing to her bump.

"We'll get the cave ready for the birth, right away," Bael promised Charlotte. "We'll make it comfortable as possible for you and Jillian."

"I'll run you out to the cave when the time comes," Zed said. "Fetch supplies. Check up on you every once in a while to make sure you don't need anything."

"It sounds like you've thought this through, which I appreciate. Any other questions?"

"I've been having really vivid nightmares," Jillian told her. "A lot of them involve me giving birth to a Jersey Devil-type creature, who then disappears into the treasure cave and steals all of Bael's fancy Egyptian art."

Charlotte patted her hand. "Well, from what I understand you have been dealing with some pretty high stress levels lately, like above average, potential apocalyptical consequences. I think you're just processing everything now that you know the situation is settled."

"That could be true," Jillian conceded.

"But if you start thinking that you're dreaming something prophetic, let me know," Charlotte insisted. "It's a *magique* world, stranger things have happened."

～

THAT AFTERNOON, CHARLOTTE WALKED TO THE PIE SHOP PERFECTLY happy with her move to Mystic Bayou. Everybody seemed so hopeful here, ready for the future, when the outside world seemed so afraid of it. It was enough to make her consider staying here long-term, just so she could be a part of that.

She walked into Bathtilda's Sweet Shoppe, an ancient wood structure with a pressed tin roof and walls painted white and emerald green. Mismatched cake stands were arranged along the long, polished counter, with Siobhan's pie creations on display through the glass domes. Chocolate-rhubarb, the strangely mouth-watering house specialty, had a special place on the back, near a mirror veined with gold. The seventies style looking glass was a bit out of place in the classic diner arrangement, with the weathered green vinyl booths and black-and-white tile floor, but overall, it was welcoming and comfortable.

Charlotte scanned the shop. She could only assume the tall, stately woman with the high cheekbones and gold clips in her iron gray hair was Bathtilda. Jillian had told her that Bathtilda was one of the few Boone relatives who was "neutral" in terms of speaking to Bael. While Bathtilda didn't attend the wedding, she also didn't do anything to prevent the ceremony—which was more than could be said for some of Bael's uncles—and she'd closed the shop so Siobhan could cover the pie catering. Bathtilda stood at the register, filling out forms. She had a lot of business acumen, Jillian told her, but no real baking skill. She was smart enough to let Siobhan run the kitchen, while she stuck to paperwork and ordering supplies.

And apparently, it worked, if the crowded shop was any indication. Every seat was filled with people blissfully digging into chocolate rhubarb, lemon meringue, apple crumble and more. Every seat, that was, except for the one across from Leonard O'Donnell.

Despite this being one of the few restaurants in town, she noticed there was no real food on any of the tables. There was bacon served with some of the apple pie, and cheese and even an arugula salad with what she thought was a pear custard pie. But no full meals. Suddenly, she was wondering how everybody in the Bayou was so healthy if all they ate were sweets.

She heard a throat clearing to her left, from behind the counter. It was nice, having other fairy folk around, for no other reason than there were other people around the same height. Siobhan peered into her eyes. "I see you, *zana* of the forest."

"Brownie of the kitchen," Charlotte replied, inclining her head.

Siobhan smirked. "My people cover far more than the kitchen."

Charlotte gestured airily. "But there are kitchens in so many different places."

"Clever," Siobhan said, narrowing her eyes. "Now, what to serve you. You could be a difficult case... I'm going to give you cherry macaroon pie."

"I've never heard of it, but I think I'd be a fool to doubt you," Charlotte said.

Siobhan lifted a glass dome and cut a large slice of a deep red pie dotted with bits of toasted coconut topping.

"Now, go over there and sit with the O'Donnell boy and in a few minutes, I'll come over and you can tell me that's the best thing you've ever eaten," Siobhan said.

Charlotte replied, "Oh, I don't know. Leonard might want to have his lunch alone and—"

Siobhan lifted a small, bony hand to stop her objections. "That's how things are done around here. You share your table. If you want to eat alone, you order to-go."

"I don't think he likes me very much," Charlotte said.

"Then *he* should have ordered his pie to-go," Siobhan told her.

Charlotte carried her plate over to Leonard's table, feeling very much like the new girl traversing a middle school cafeteria. She could see his long frame go rigid as she approached and her heart sank. So far, all of Leonard's reactions to her had been indi-rect–something she could chalk up to coincidence or misunder-standing. She honestly didn't know how she would get through an outright rejection.

"Leonard, would you mind if I joined you?" Charlotte asked.

He glanced up at her, his dark eyes practically churning with indecision. "Hi Charlotte."

There was an achingly awkward moment where she seriously considered turning around and eating her pie while standing at the counter.

He cleared his throat. "Sure. Have a seat."

She slid into the booth, setting her pie in front of her. But before she could enjoy what was sure to be a pastry gift from the heavens, she wanted to clear the bullshit from the table. "Have I done something to offend you?"

"No," he said, looking startled. "Oh, no. Why would you think that?"

"It's just that I feel like you're avoiding me and I couldn't help but notice that we were fine until I told you I'm a fae and if it's

38

because you're uncomfortable around me, I get it. I don't even blame you for it. Some people get uncomfortable around fairies. But I'd rather just get it out in the open so we don't have to dance around it," Charlotte said.

"I'm so sorry." He pinched the bridge of his nose. "It's not that...it's that you mentioned cursing when you talked about your abilities...and yeah, it's made me–I'd like to use the word 'wary' but clearly, I've just been rude."

She winced. "So, I'm assuming by 'cursing' you don't mean obscenity."

The corners of his generous mouth lifted for a moment. "No. I know it's none of my business and asking this is...I just..." he swallowed heavily. "Have you ever cursed anybody?"

"Just once," she said, pinching her lips together. "It's not a very pretty story, but trust me when I say he deserved it."

A chill seemed to run down his spine, rattling him so hard his teeth chattered. He gripped the edge of the table and took a deep breath. He closed his eyes and the pity she felt for him bordered on heartbreak. This was the reason she'd only cursed one person in her lifetime, why her mother had never done it. Not once. Because the ripples of the magic laid on a bloodline never stopped hurting people. The lesson was too heavy and came at too great a price.

"And to make another assumption, that little zing of magic I feel when you're around... that's not static electricity, is it?" Charlotte asked.

He shook his head.

"How far back does it go?"

"1813." he sighed. "It's funny that a lot of cursed families don't know exactly when their ancestor messed up on a catastrophic level, but I know the date by heart."

She nodded, cutting into her pie just to give her something to do. "That's strong magic, to be passed so far down the line. What did your family do to make a fairy that angry?"

Leonard sat back in the booth. "Well, from what I've been told, we were once considered sort of well to do back in Ireland. The family owned a lot of land, were kind to their tenants, and generally well-regarded and productive. But there's a prick in every rosebush, and that was my many-times-great uncle Seamus. I've seen the portrait...well, the ones that later generations didn't vandalize. He was handsome, probably would have been considered your classic Prince Charming if he hadn't been such an ass."

"You'd be surprised how often the two traits are combined," she told him, taking a bite of pie. The moment the sweet, fruity symphony of flavors hit her tongue, she reached out and grabbed Leonard's hand for support. It was like lying on a bed made with freshly hung linen, the smell of the sun and the wind wafting up from the sheets. It was peace and pleasure all in one.

She opened her eyes and saw she was still holding hands with Leonard across the table. She smiled sheepishly. "Sorry."

"It's a fairly common response," he assured her, though he seemed reluctant to loosen his hold on her fingers. Her hand looked so small in his, but he was cradling it like it was something delicate and precious. She could feel the magic that lived on his skin, as much a part of him as his pores, but it was unnatural and wrong. This wasn't him. This awkward clumsiness was like a pair of shackles, holding him back. To his credit, the moment she pulled away, he let go.

Charlotte cleared her throat. "I'll try to keep the obscene noises to a minimum."

"I don't mind so much," he admitted, his cheeks flushing. When she giggled, he went on with his story. "Anyway, from what my grandad told me, Seamus O'Donnell just loved mocking people he didn't consider quite up to his snuff. People who had less than him. People who weren't as 'polished.' In April 1813, there was a grand party for a young lady who was 'coming out,' one of the other well-to-do families in the county. She tripped over the hem of her gown coming down the stairs into the ballroom, laid flat out on her face for her own party. Poor girl. Well, of course, Seamus started laughing and making stupid jokes about her tripping over her own 'oversized feet,' asking if the musicians had any music fit for a horse to clomp along to. For weeks afterward, he would make whickering noises if he saw her out in town. That sort of thing."

"What a jackass." She sighed.

"I know!" he exclaimed, digging into his own slice of chocolate cream pie. "Well, apparently, as rich as they were, the girl's family kept to the old ways; leaving out milk and seeds and pretty stones on their windowsill for the fae folk, building their home with as little iron as possible, singing to the trees whenever they were outside. So their daughter was considered blessed. She had her very own self-appointed fairy godmother. And she didn't appreciate seeing her beloved goddaughter mocked. She knew her goddaughter had only tripped because she was nervous and she wanted Seamus to know what it was like, not to be able to control your own body when your stress was high. So she came to the estate and told him all he had to do was apologize. And of course, he refused because in his opinion, the young lady in question shouldn't take herself so seriously. The fairy was so angered by his lack of remorse that she cursed him, so that the more nervous he became, the more he fumbled. And because she wanted the whole family to know the injury Seamus had done to her goddaughter's family, ruining what was an important social occasion for them, she cursed the entire line. Oh, and if the O'Donnells tried to do anything to remove the curse–besides Seamus sincerely apologizing–it would get three times worse."

"Oof, that is...incredibly clever and insidious," Charlotte marveled, her lips pulling back in a grimace. "I mean, I don't want to sound like I admire it. But, wow."

Come to think of it, she'd never heard of a curse working that way. But she wasn't exactly an expert in this arena. She made a mental note to call her mother, who was much more knowledge-able about these things.

"As someone who's lived with it for years, I can assure you that it was very effective," he told her. "But people here understand. Whenever I drop something, all I have to say is 'fairy curse' and they just nod and shake their heads and say nothing else. You don't get that out in the real world. Or at least, you didn't before the Pope Lick Monster incident. Anyway, all Seamus had to do was apologize, and the whole family would have had a different destiny. Idiot Seamus didn't believe her, despite her explaining the how's and the why's in great detail in front of his entire family. At first, he wasn't worried, after all he was so self-assured he never got nervous. It started off small, dropping something when he was talking to a pretty girl, tripping when he was walking down the street. But it was a crack in his armor and his nerves got worse and the accidents got more serious. The family fortunes waned because it takes a steady, clear mind to run a large farm and it's hard to keep steady when *anything* could go wrong at any moment. Seamus never repented, even when his family begged him to–because somehow, his pride was more important than admitting that he'd done a stupid, cruel thing. Eventually, he was run over in the street by a carriage, and there was a pretty sparse crowd at his funeral."

"It feels mean to say 'good.' And yet…" Charlotte noted.

"Well, the curse didn't end with him, obviously. The family lost the farm, well before the Great Famine set in. We moved to Amer-ica, hoping that maybe distance from the fae would weaken the curse. Well, it took a couple of tries for us to move to America. One of my great-great-uncles fell off the gangway of a steamer ship to Boston, and drowned, and the rest of the family chickened out and went back to Galway for a few years. We managed to eke out a life here, but we've suffered a lot of tragedy along the way. A lot of us end up single because no one wants to date the guy who dumps half a punchbowl on them at the school dance. I guess

42

that's another added smack from the curse. If the bloodline isn't ended by accidental death, we'll blunder our way right out of the gene pool," Leonard said.

He was saying it with a light-hearted tone, like he was joking, but she could feel the helpless grief in him. She took his hand again. The static electricity of their touching had been replaced by a pleasant, warm thrum, like the echo of a bell. She very much doubted that Leonard deserved the curse that had been leveled on him, for his empathy alone. But she supposed that was the point of the curse, to teach the O'Donnell line a little compassion for people who were struggling. The curse had done its work. She only wished the original cursing fairy had added a loophole to let more deserving generations out of it.

Suddenly, the echo of the bell wasn't just a feeling throughout her body, but a noise coming from her purse. Her phone was chiming. She shot him an apologetic look, but then his phone buzzed as well. He took the phone out of his pocket while she reached for her bag. Her screen showed an email from the League office stating that the department head meeting scheduled for the next day had been moved to that afternoon—in fact, it was scheduled to start in twenty minutes.

"Oh, for fuck's sake," he grumbled.

"Watch your language in my restaurant, young man!" Bathtilda warned him sharply.

"What is happening?" Charlotte asked.

"Jessica, my archnemesis, has moved the department head meeting."

Charlotte snickered. "You have an archnemesis?"

"Yeah, I know that sounds weird," he said, pulling a few bills out of his wallet and tucking it under the napkin dispenser.

"No, not really. I mean, I think most people have an archnemesis, real or imagined. They just don't come out and *admit* it," Charlotte said.

"Well, I do, and she just moved the department head meeting

up twenty-four hours, which means she's up to something," he grumbled. "Either she's counting on me not having the necessary paperwork and agendas prepped so she can embarrass me or she's planning to have prepped everything herself so she can come out looking like a hero; which is unlikely, because I password protected all of the agendas on the shared server. And she doesn't have the information necessary to create her own. *And* she doesn't know that I prepped and printed everything yesterday and locked the copies in my desk drawer."

Leonard shrugged. She noted that he sprang to his feet, offering his hand, without moving in his usual, stiff manner. Charlotte lifted a brow as he went to the counter to tell Siobhan that the meeting had been moved and they would need "the usual order" that afternoon instead. Siobhan only gave him a befuddled look as he dashed out of the shop.

"I think he's confused," Siobhan told Charlotte.

Charlotte dropped some bills in the tip jar, smiling apologetically. "Administrative work involves more espionage activities than I expected."

4

LEONARD

*S*ometimes, it paid to be highly organized.

The moment he walked into his office and found the meeting agendas still locked in his desk, he knew that Jessica's attempt at a meeting coup failed. Within seconds of his butt hitting his desk chair, she was standing in front of him, seething. "Where are the agendas for today's meeting, Leonard?'

"You mean tomorrow's meeting?" Leonard asked.

Jessica sniffed. "It was moved to this afternoon because of a conflict in Mr. Lancaster's schedule."

"That you arranged?" Leonard deadpanned.

"It's not my fault that you can't keep up with a fast-paced office environment." Jessica smirked at him and Leonard itched to do something really awful to her desk.

Leonard glanced around the empty lobby, where the most active object was a ficus leaf bobbing in a gust of air-conditioning. Even in the midst of his confrontation with Jessica, regret and resentment gnawed at his belly. It was Jessica's fault his conversation with Charlotte had been cut short. Despite the otherworldly nature that, frankly, set him on edge, he found he liked the midwife quite a bit. He liked how efficient she was, how she cut to the heart of the matter at hand, how quickly the people he admired trusted her with the most important things in their lives. She had a competence about her that made people want to hand her those things. And if Jessica could just calm the hell down, he might have been able to build a better understanding with her.

"It is against League policy to password protect documents on a shared server. You don't have the authorization to hide information from me," Jessica said.

Leonard unlocked the drawer and piled the agendas onto his desk. Then he reached into the top drawer and pulled out a sheet of paper signed by Sonja. "Authorization from the director of operations, to use my discretion to protect information as long as I share it to her private server."

Jessica snatched the paper out of his hand and tossed it in the garbage. He rolled his eyes and pulled out another copy, which was laminated. "I also have a digital version saved on my phone."

"I'll carry those into the meeting room, thank you," she said, holding her gloved hand out expectantly as he locked the drawers again. It was sad that he had to lock them, but obviously it was the right choice.

"You are really choosing some weird ways to try to make a good impression," he told Jessica, stepping around her and walking out of the door towards the conference trailer. Part of him felt bad for Jessica, because obviously she was more than just "a little distressed" about her changing role. But there was more than enough work to go around in the Bayou. She could thrive if she wasn't trying to swipe what she saw as the "highest profile" tasks. He was going to have to have another conversation with Sonja because Jessica was coming across as a little unhinged–and unhinged administrative assistants left unsupervised was a bad thing in the Bayou.

Leonard walked into the conference room to find Zed studying a poster sized chart pinned to the walls. Leonard had spent the better part of a day getting those printed and arranging them just so. Things were changing fast in the Bayou and he wondered if Zed, whose family had lived here for centuries, resented the League and its impact on his home. Jillian had originally been welcomed into the town because cooperation with the League meant much-needed resources, like funding for the clinic and new roads. Were those things worth potential exposure to the outside world?

"Zed, what are you doing here?" Leonard asked.

"Hey, bud. Just looking at a chart of our population forecasts. Jillian asked me to join tomorrow's meeting about the issues facing the town post-Pope Lick Monster," Zed replied. Zed gave Jessica a disapproving look as she walked through the door. She scowled when she saw Leonard was placing agendas in front of each seat.

Alex, Jillian, Sonja, Dani, Rob, Adam, and the other department heads filed in, each giving Leonard a friendly wave. Will walked in with Charlotte and sent Sonja a very "professional" eyebrow wiggle from across the room. Sonja rolled her eyes as she took her seat near Alex, but she was grinning. Zed was far less professional, sweeping Dani into a kiss that belonged on the front of a romance novel. Probably involving an MMA fighter. Bael had no role in this meeting whatsoever, but was hovering behind Jillian as if she could collapse or burst into flames any minute. Either one was possible, but she'd done the flame thing before and it was always a crowd-pleaser.

This was one of the things he liked best about working in the Bayou, the people. (Well, except for Jessica, who was the worst.) He had *friends* here, something he'd never quite managed in his hometown in Ohio. He was contributing, making the world a better place for people—something that would have been more difficult in his original field as a geologist. Unless you managed to find an enormous secret volcano and stop it from erupting, there weren't a lot of "save the world" opportunities in geology. He'd already had at least two in this job.

"Well, glad to have you here," Leonard told Zed. "Siobhan should be delivering the pies any minute."

Leonard checked the time on his phone. Frankly, it was strange that the pies weren't there already. Even with the late notice, Siobhan always had a reserve of pies in case of a rush.

"Oh, I cancelled that order," Jessica said. "Pie just seems like a heavy, messy food for an after-lunch meeting. I got a fruit plate and some gluten-free muffins instead."

Absolute silence.

Every single person in the room was staring at Jessica in horror. Zed actually clutched his chest like he was having a heart attack.

"What have you done?" Dani whispered.

"Do you think we come to these meetings for the *fruit?*" Ivy Portenoy demanded. When Alex's brows rose, she added, "OK, sure we come here to for important Bayou matters and to make the world a better place…but mostly, it's the pie!"

"I think it's the gluten-free muffins that's pushing her over the edge," Sonja murmured.

"It's a healthier option!" Jessica insisted. "There's no reason for the League to pay exorbitant prices for locally made pies. They're not even artisanal! I think Siobhan uses *lard* in her crust!"

Zed leveled a look at Alex. "We need to have a talk."

Jillian cleared her throat, struggling to keep a pleasant expression on her face. "Leonard, please offer Siobhan our deepest apologies and assure her that order will not be changed again in the near future."

"Got it," Leonard leapt up from his chair and jogged across the street. No wonder Bathtilda was so snippy with him in the pie shoppe earlier. She'd thought he cancelled the League's regular meeting order without explanation. Siobhan met him at the door, smirking, carrying a stack of pie boxes.

"Siobhan, I wouldn't have run out of here earlier if I'd known she cancelled the order. I'm so sorry," Leonard said.

"Sonja already texted," she said. "Apologies accepted. Also, I had Bathtilda add a twenty percent pain-in-my-ass fee to the invoice."

"You text?" he asked, tilting his head as he stared at her.

"I'm ancient, not outdated," she replied, handing him the boxes. "Get with the times, Leonard."

"Make it a thirty percent pain-in-the-ass fee," he told her, before running back across Main Street. He could hear her cackling behind him.

He rushed into the conference room, carefully placing the boxes on the end of the table and passing out plates and napkins. Zed was midsentence, sounding much more like an elected official than he normally did, "We're just not ready for the numbers Dr. Assf- Aspern is projecting. We already have *drole* living in an improvised RV park at the end of Main Street. Theresa's been fielding calls from businesses wanting to talk to our Chamber of Commerce. We don't have a Chamber of Commerce, less you count the Boone Family. And giving them more power is the last thing we need. No offense, Bael."

Bael shrugged.

"And as much as we want to welcome anyone and everyone who wants to live in the Bayou, we're not ready for a massive influx of new residents," Zed lamented. "We don't have the infrastructure, the public works, the supply chain, the stores, anything to support a population boom like this."

"If it helps, Bonita De Los Santos said that several tour companies have inquired about setting up post office boxes. Tourism dollars will only help local economy," Adam noted, pulling out a chart he'd printed.

Dani cupped her hands together, a ball of light forming between her palms. It was her usual method of dealing with Adam when he tried to take over meetings, waffling on about

49

how he was single-handedly saving Mystic Bayou's financial future.

"People want to do *tours?*" Zed exclaimed, shaking his head. "Do they realize how insulting that is? We're not a zoo!"

"Maybe instead of letting people wander through the Bayou unsupervised, we arrange some sort of seminar?" Jillian suggested, laying a hand on Zed's arm. "Guest speakers and lectures all in one contained place, like a visitor's center? Where they can't do any damage and it's sort of contained?"

"We don't have a visitor's center, Jillian," Zed replied, "Or hotels or apartments to rent. And the last thing we want is for a housing development to spring up near the old rift site or something. And how do we feed all these people without running the grocery store empty every other day?"

"What about pop up stores?" Sonja suggested. "Or helping the grocery establish delivery trucks? You know they're a big hit in the outside world, and it would provide a much-needed service for older residents. Bael could maybe avoid pulling over poor Emily McAinsley every time she drives into town."

"I think Emily and I would both appreciate that," Bael muttered. "But construction takes time around here and these temporary fixes to long-term issues are going to involve a lot of trailers. That could be a problem, come hurricane season."

"We need engineers," Zed said. "Electrical, sewage, roads, all of the things that communities need to provide for their citizens on a larger scale. We need to catch up."

"So with the engineering and construction types moving to town, that's even more people," Will mused. "People who will need the housing and food and all the stuff we mentioned, plus medical care, a firehouse, a real courthouse facility. All of the things you need when people get into the mishaps involved in being people. We may have to build a hospital."

"Mystic Bayou can't stay the same," Dani said gently, kissing Zed's cheek. "That was never an option."

"But we can keep the changes from being destructive," Zed muttered. "Keep the local businesses from getting run out of town. Keep the cost of living from getting so high the families who have always lived here can't afford it anymore."

"We're here to help any way we can," Alex promised.

"We're gonna have to add another stoplight, huh?" Zed asked.

"That will make three!" Bael crowed, raising his hands in triumph.

~

LEONARD PULLED HIS TRUCK DOWN THE GRAVEL DRIVE TO THE *maison de fous*, a strange mishmashed house on the water that Will and Sonja were renting from the town. Called the House of Fools by the locals, it consisted of several faded blue-gray stories, topped by a copper cupola, green with age.

As Leonard carried his offering of flowers and a bottle of wine down the drive, he could see mason jar lanterns strung over a dock that extended from under the "ground floor" to the water. Guests were sprawled in a ring of comfortable looking, mismatched chairs, watching the twilight bloom. Witch bottles glowed to life in the trees, giving the small gathering a festive air. Bael had Jillian seated in a heavily cushioned Adirondack chair, rubbing her feet. Dani was perched in Zed's lap, chatting with Jillian while sipping a can of ginger ale. Will was burning something on the grill and couldn't have looked happier, while Cordelia Canton gave him pointers on proper grilling techniques.

Charlotte was standing at the end of the dock, talking to Will's brother, Jon, while they drank beer. A sudden and sharp pang of jealousy speared right through Leonard's chest, and it shamed him. Charlotte seemed like the kind of lady that deserved someone like Jon, a selkie like his brother, who was a decent enough person to have earned Sonja's good opinion–which wasn't easy. Also, Jon didn't have a curse hanging over his head.

Maybe fate could have been a little kinder by not pairing Charlotte with someone so broodily and sensitively handsome–right in front of Leonard's face. But he'd gotten used to this sort of kick in the teeth from fate.

It was the first time Leonard hadn't seen her in her sensible scrubs and he was having a hard time not staring at her lithe figure in a floral sundress. The cool blue fabric brought out the caramel highlights in her hair and made her eyes seem even larger. She turned those eyes towards his and smiled sweetly. He dropped his gaze to the ground, the water, anything that would make it seem that he wasn't staring at her like a big creep.

Step One In Getting Through a Potentially Disastrous Social Occasion at Your Boss's House: Stop staring at your boss' guests.

"Leonard! I'm so glad you could make it!" Sonja exclaimed as Leonard handed her the wine and flowers. "This is so sweet of you! Nice bottle, too."

"Thanks for inviting me, Sonja."

"Well, we really haven't had any sort of party here since we moved in," Sonja replied. "Too many near catastrophes. Besides, we had to welcome Charlotte to town properly. And make up for that nightmare meeting."

"And thank you for not inviting Jessica or Alex, even though it will probably be awkward at work tomorrow," he said quietly.

She shrugged nonchalantly, then told him, "Go make yourself comfortable."

Leonard grabbed a beer from the cooler and stood on the outside of the group, just watching the interactions. It was his normal MO during parties. There were too many opportunities for him to spill something or knock something over.

Jon followed Sonja inside, probably to fetch Charlotte another beer or pearls from the bottom of the sea or something super-impressive and romantic. Dani announced a need to visit the ladies room, leaving Zed to fold Cordelia into his arms and press a brotherly kiss to her forehead. Her boyfriend, Brendan, just rolled his eyes and shook his head.

"I don't need to remind you that if you hurt my Cordelia, I can and will snap you like kindling, Irish!" Zed called. Brendan replied with something rude in Gaelic—which Leonard didn't speak, but he knew international profanity when he heard it.

"Are Zed and Cordelia related?" Charlotte asked Leonard.

Leonard shook his head. "No, but he adopted her formally—or as formally as a bear can—after she moved here. There was forehead-licking involved, that's all I know."

"Zed seems like a very nice man, but I would like my forehead to remain un-licked," Charlotte told him.

"I would say that's reasonable," he conceded. "But he doesn't just go around adopting people willy-nilly. Cordelia was in desperate need of family."

"Well, that's sweet of him," she said. "Aside from the licking. So, your family, what are they like?"

"Haven't we already talked about my family?" he replied. "Pretty normal, aside from the curse. What about yours? It has to be more interesting, what with the fairy history."

"This is going to sound awful," she said, cringing.

"I doubt it," he said. "Given my own cursed state, keep in mind that I'm in no place to judge."

Charlotte's brow wrinkled, as if she was trying to apologize for the words coming out of her mouth. "I tried moving back home after I graduated and working with my mother. But it didn't work out."

That was her big secret? Being unable to work with her mom? Leonard shook his head. "Well, yeah, working with family can be a nightmare. I worked at my dad's garage every summer from sixth grade to high school graduation. I don't think we had a civil dinner conversation in the summertime until I got my first lab job. You spend all day together and then you go home together. Little resentments build up, things you were supposed to do and didn't, things you wish they wouldn't do and they never seem to stop."

"Yes, exactly that," she gasped, clutching his arm as if he was some sort of lifeline of understanding. Leonard tried not to sigh from the warm sensation winding out from his arm to his chest, just under his heart. Surely, sighing in the middle of a conversation, like you'd just slid into a hot bath, would be rude and off-putting.

"Don't get me wrong," Charlotte said. "My parents are amazing people. They're kind and supportive and they love me so much. So even when I moved into my own place, the phone was just ringing all of the time and anything became an excuse for me to come over to their place. By the time we were about a year into a practice together, I realized I needed some space. The League offered me a job and while I frequently call and video chat with my parents every Saturday, I try to limit my visits to Christmas."

His eyes narrowed as he stared at her. She grimaced. "I knew that was going to sound bad."

He laughed. "No, I'm just trying to figure out how you get away with it. Do you have any idea how awful holidays can be when your entire family gets more and more clumsy the more stressed out they are? We've never gotten a turkey all the way to the table. *Never.*"

"I would imagine it's pretty bad," she said, nodding. "But yesterday, during that really weird meeting, you managed to run across the street without any problems, while carrying a bunch of pies. It was practically a Three Stooges set-up and...nothing."

He scoffed. "Well, yeah, but I wasn't nervous then. It wasn't my screw up. It was Jessica's. I was just trying to fix it and help Sonja and Jillian. I love helping Sonja and Jillian. I don't get stressed out doing what I love."

She grinned at him and he actually felt his heart catch...which honestly, sort of hurt, but it was worth it to know that he was the one who brought that joy to her face. She clinked her bottle against his.

"I know exactly what you mean," Charlotte said.

In that moment, Leonard decided he wanted Charlotte McBee, badly, and the thought of even trying to woo her made him *very* nervous. And he was in a lot of trouble.

5

CHARLOTTE

*C*harlotte enjoyed a rare weekend morning off, cleaning the Silver Stork and doing her grocery shopping, securing a PO Box from the very subtly nosy Mrs. De Los Santos, and other adulting chores. She felt very productive when she sat down for her weekly video call with her parents. Now that she'd established herself as an adult with a lot of space between her household (mobile as it was) and her parents, their relationship was a lot better. She found herself looking forward to their weekend calls. It had been freeing to talk to Leonard the night before, and for him to understand how she felt about her family.

While Will had been none-too-subtle in introducing Charlotte to his perfectly nice and "extremely single" brother, Jon, Charlotte had spent most of the prior evening talking to Leonard. She thought maybe that was Sonja's aim because the more time she spent with Leonard, the happier Sonja became–but Will got glummer and glummer. When the evening wound to a close and Leonard offered to drive her back to her trailer, Sonja's smirk was almost indecent.

Leonard had driven like a grandma on the winding, twisting roads back to the town. But she didn't have the heart to tease him about it. She sensed that he didn't want to make some random mistake while driving and hurt her. He was trying to protect her from the consequences of his curse. It was sweet, really, like most things about Leonard.

She couldn't help but watch his elegant hands moving carefully on the steering wheel and remember the way he'd darted across Main Street. His long legs carried him with purpose and confidence and the memory of it had her squirming in her seat. A lot of aspects of Leonard were pretty attractive, but seeing him move like a man on a mission? Even if that mission was retrieving forsaken pie, well, she was just happy to be on the receiving end of it.

Charlotte wondered if he used that sort of care and determination...everywhere.

He'd parked far enough from the Silver Stork that he couldn't possibly risk hitting it. Then he carefully stepped around the car and opened her door, taking her hand and helping her out of her seat with aching slowness. She knew it wasn't particularly enlightened, to get hot and bothered over being treated like spun glass. But she'd worked so hard for so long, taking care of other people. And even though she *loved* that work, it was nice having someone take care of her. She squeezed her fingers around Leonard's as they approached her "front step."

"Big plans over the weekend?" he'd asked.

"The Saturday phone call and errands," she said. "Taking Sunday as my day of rest, though I'm never really able to relax, just in case someone goes into labor."

"Well, you should!" he said. "Relax, I mean. You can't take care of anybody if you're all drained and tired."

When she smiled at him, he took both her hands in his.

"When does your confinement with Jillian start?" he asked, turning those hands over and staring at them like they were something precious.

"Probably next week," she said. "It all depends on Jillian, of course."

"Well, I'll be in my office, unless Jessica tries to move my desk into the parking lot," he said. "If you ever want to meet for pie or take a drive out to the old rift site, I'd be happy to take you."

It was the way he *asked*, not demanding like so many other men, but making it entirely her choice, that had her craning up to kiss him. She'd gone up on her tippy-toes and he'd still had to duck his head to meet her lips. And she could feel his mouth curving up, even as it brushed against hers. Those long arms she admired wrapped around her and lifted her just a little bit, making her laugh into his lips.

"I'll call you," she told him, before turning to unlock her door.

"You don't have my number," Leonard replied.

"Sonja gave it to me," she'd chirped.

"I love my boss," he sighed as she popped her door open and closed it behind her.

Charlotte was so caught in this memory, in the memory of how soft and warm his lips felt against hers, that she'd very nearly forgotten that she was supposed to call her parents at noon. She hit "call" on her video chat app and pulled her plate of *boudin* and rice dressing from Clarissa Berend in front of her. So far, this was her favorite contribution from the Bayou mamas, but she would never say so because then she would get flooded with Tupperware from Clarissa's competition. Her mother insisted on eating lunch together during these calls, just so Lizzie knew that Charlotte was "keeping body and soul together."

Hank McBee's rounded, ruddy face appeared on the screen, far too close to the camera. "Hey, Daddy, all I'm seeing is forehead."

"Oh, right." Her dad leaned away from the laptop and waved merrily. "Hey there, shortcake. Your mama's in the shower. Misty McGee had her twins last night. Mama didn't get back until the wee hours."

Charlotte shuddered, suddenly glad to be dealing with just one baby at a time, even if the baby was part dragon.

"So how's it going in Name Redacted Bayou?" Hank said.

"Very funny," she sighed. Her father had been calling her his "the spy who delivered babies" since she swore her parents to secrecy over her location.

"In all seriousness, I know it's insulting to your role as a professional when I fuss over my grown daughter, but I'm worried about you, sweetheart," he said. "If you think that the mood in town is shifting, you high-tail it for home."

"I couldn't leave my patients," she replied. "Besides, I'd be better protected here than I would be at home, with all of the League resources we have here. If anything, I'd want you and Mama to come here. I don't think our neighbors are going to take too well to the idea that you and Mama have been lyin' to them all this time."

"You let me worry about that," he said. "So how are things in the eye of the storm?"

"It's going well. Busy, but the people are really nice."

Charlotte was smiling dreamily, thinking of Leonard, before she realized it.

Her daddy's brown eyes narrowed and he grinned. "Any one person in particular?"

Dang it. She never had been able to hide anything from her father. He may not have had supernatural powers, but he could sniff out a lie like a freaking bloodhound.

"Maybe," she said, her cheeks flushing. "We've just met, so who knows."

"Well, sometimes you just know" he said. "And sometimes, people don't figure out they made a mistake until they're half-way down the aisle. You don't have to rush things. Hell, it took me months before I convinced your mama to go on a date with me."

"Yeah, I wouldn't go around telling people that," Charlotte told him.

"It was called *courtship*, back then, shortcake," Hank said.

She pursed her lips. "Mmmhmmm."

"Is he a nice boy?" her father asked.

"He's a nice *man*," she replied, snickering when he pulled a disgusted face. "He's perfectly sweet and downright gentlemanly."

"Is he like you and Mama? Or like me?" Hank asked.

It was a delicate question. Charlotte's grandmother hadn't been entirely thrilled with Hank as a mate for Lizzie. There had always been some hope that Lizzie would meet another fae, but still, Grandma wanted Lizzie to be happy. And Hank made Lizzie very happy.

"He's human, but there are complications," Charlotte said.

Hank arched an eyebrow. "Does he have horns like that Pope Lick Monster fella?"

Charlotte laughed. "No, other complications. I'll talk about it when Mama gets on the call. That way I just say it all at once."

"Well, speak of the devil," he said, ducking away as a hand came into frame and lightly smacked his shoulder.

"That man," her mama sighed as she sat at the kitchen table. Charlotte watched Daddy make her mother a mug of steaming coffee, doctored just the way she liked it with three sugars.

"Daddy said you had a late night," Charlotte said.

"Oh, it was fine. Your daddy just worries if I'm out past sunset. How are you settling in?"

"Fine," Charlotte insisted. "It's a little strange, so many *magique* living in one place, but nice."

Lizzie rolled her eyes and sipped her coffee. "What a time to be alive, eh?"

"She's seeing someone!" Daddy called from the stove, where he was frying eggs. "And he's 'complicated.'"

"Thank you, Daddy," Charlotte muttered.

"Complicated how?" Lizzie asked. "Honey, is he married? You know better!"

"Mama, he's not married!" Charlotte laughed. "Though, that

might be preferable. His whole line's been fae-cursed. He gets progressively more clumsy the more stressed out he gets. Apparently, it ruined his career in the science labs, so now he's working as an administrator for the big muckity-mucks here in the Bayou."

Lizzie sat back in her chair. "Oh, that is a nasty bit of magic."

"It really is," Charlotte agreed.

"Have you offered to remove it?" her mother asked.

"Apparently, the only way to remove it was for the cursed ancestor to apologize to the girl he hurt. Which is impossible now, since that guy's been dead for a century or two," Charlotte replied. "And if anybody else tries to remove it, it will get three times worse."

Lizzie frowned. "Well, the apology was the only way for the original casting fairy to remove the curse, sure. That was the condition she was allowed to apply to the magic, as the creator."

"I'm sensing a 'but' here," Charlotte said.

"Well, magic is different for everybody, but the basic laws are still the same. You couldn't just create magic without end, echoing on forever. That's not how it works. It's like the terms and conditions in contracts. If you can apply a clause, you can remove it," Lizzie said.

"That is a sad and pragmatic way to describe magic," Daddy told her, sliding a plate of buttered toast in front of her.

"It sounds like the fairy who cursed the line just wanted to make sure the family never consulted a magic practitioner to undo her work," Lizzie said.

"Leonard's family never tried to remove the curse, because they were too afraid...so they stayed cursed forever. Wow, that fairy godmother was *mean*," Charlotte marveled.

"The power of belief," Lizzie said, jerking her shoulders and biting into her toast.

"And if I wanted to remove the curse, how would I do that?" Charlotte said.

Her mother's expression became even more discomfited.

Giving a baby a blessing only took words and good intentions. But undoing another fairy's curse? That was a totally different matter. The Popescu-McBees didn't practice magic, usually. There was too much that could go wrong in the process of birthing to add the complications of ritual. But Lizzie had a treasure trove of her ancestors' books and magical tools hidden away in the attic and she'd never shied away from learning. Charlotte, on the other hand, feared what sort of person she might become if she had shortcuts in a world that was already filled with them. So she'd left the studying to Mama, promising herself she would pick it up in a far-off "someday."

"Someday" had a way of sneaking up on people, human or fae.

Lizzie chewed her toast thoughtfully. "Well, the best 'catch-all' I know to remove curses is to counteract it with a potion made from very powerful magical ingredients. I mean the magical equivalent of turpentine, *very strong*. You're going to need to base it on something with real oomph from an ancient magical creature–hair from a unicorn's mane, a phoenix's talon, scales from the ouroboros's tail, a dragon's eggshell–

Charlotte perked up. "A dragon's eggshell?"

"You have access to a dragon's eggshell?" Mama asked quietly.

Charlotte paused, wondering how much she could say without violating patient confidentiality laws. "Let's just say that I *might* have access to a dragon's eggshell, and the shell will have a little phoenix DNA in there, too. Would that help or hurt?"

Lizzie's blue eyes went wide as she nearly choked on her toast, but she recovered gracefully. "Well, there's no guarantee, of course. It all depends on your intention, how the ingredients interact, and whether your subject deserves to have the curse removed in the first place. Magic is a living thing and makes judgments. It doesn't tolerate intervention on the behalf of jackasses."

"That's beautiful." Daddy laid two eggs sunnyside-up on Mama's plate. "Is that Shakespeare?"

"Smartass!" Mama swatted at him, grinning as he poured her

more coffee. "I'll look through the books to see if I can find a specific recipe."

"Well, first, I have to ask the egg-owner in question if I can borrow some. How exactly am I going to phrase that?" Charlotte said.

"Carefully." Lizzie nodded, chewing her eggs. "If I find anything, I'll email it to you."

"You're going to email the ancient potion recipe?" Charlotte gasped. "What would Granny say?"

"She would say shame on me for raising a pretentious Luddite for a daughter," Lizzie said.

Charlotte snorted. "Thanks, Mama."

"And another thing, you're going to have to tell him exactly what you're doing and what is in the potion," Lizzie said.

"Of course, I wouldn't just dose him with crushed up dragon shell without telling him," Charlotte replied. "But why?"

"Well, from what I can tell, it's all part of the process. People who have been cursed didn't have a choice in the matter. Choosing something different is a big part of changing it," Lizzie said.

"Noted," Charlotte said, digging into her plate of sausage.

"So, do you think you might bring this boy around to meet us sometime?" Lizzie asked, far too casually.

"Let me try to fix it so I can get him out of the state without a catastrophe, and we'll talk," Charlotte said.

AFTER THE CALL, CHARLOTTE MULLED OVER THIS PREDICAMENT. Before she could even consider raising Leonard's hopes about the potion, she had to ask Jillian to "borrow a cup of mystical eggshell."

But how in the hell did you even ask for that?

And as most people did in the Bayou when they had a strange

and insurmountable task in front of them, Charlotte went to Sonja.

The trick was that she had to find Sonja at a time when Leonard wasn't sitting directly outside of Sonja's office. Charlotte had to wait, watching the League administration building through her window until Leonard left for the post office. She scampered across Main Street to the League office, not even stopping when Jessica Galanis called out to her.

Sonja's brow lifted as Charlotte shut her office door behind her. Outside, Jessica rattled the handle furiously. Charlotte wedged her back against the door, gritting her teeth. "Damn, that girl is *strong*."

"Is everything OK?" Sonja demanded. "Is Jillian in labor? Wait, no, Jillian's down the hall and would have yelled for me. What's going on?

Charlotte tried to explain, but her voice was barely audible over the din of Jessica's pounding on the door. Sonja rolled her eyes and crossed the room, opening the door and nearly getting smacked in the face by Jessica's fist.

"That *woman*," Jessica spat, glaring past Sonja, "just rushed in here without an *appointment*."

"She did have an appointment with me, but as you don't manage my schedule, I didn't see fit to inform you," Sonja told Jessica.

"But—"

"Thank you, Jessica." Sonja shut the door in Jessica's face, turning to Charlotte. She sighed. "I know I should have more sympathy for her and support her as another administrative professional—but I swear to you, Leonard is the only non-evil assistant we've ever had."

"I do not like her, but I'm biased," Charlotte admitted. "Jillian's fine, by the way, to the best of my knowledge. But I have something I need to ask her and I thought I should get your advice first."

"Shoot." Sonja gave her a warm smile as she gestured to the chair across from her desk.

And suddenly, Charlotte was babbling. "Well, this is really awkward for me to have to ask. I don't even know how to start and I don't want Jillian to think I'm using her baby for my own gain–"

Sonja said kindly, "It might be better if you just got to the point, Charlotte."

"Do you think Jillian would be willing to donate some of the baby's eggshell after he or she is born?" Charlotte blurted out.

"Are you going to do some sort of weird science experiment with *them?*" Sonja asked. "Because she would have some objections to that. Oh honey, please don't turn out to be evil, we just don't have the emotional energy to deal with another supervillain."

"What?!" Charlotte exclaimed. "No. I'm trying to remove Leonard's fairy curse and my mama thinks it'll require a potion made with a dragon's eggshell."

"Oh! That's the sweetest thing I've ever heard!" Sonja cried, rounding the corner and hugging her tight. "Yes, of course, she would be willing to donate some of the eggshell to helping Leonard. We love him! And just think of how much better he would be at his job without potential disasters."

Sonja ran for the door and shouted, "Jillian!"

"What!" Charlotte exclaimed, following Sonja out of her office, past a glaring Jessica. "Wait, I wanted to approach her carefully."

"It'll be fine," Sonja assured her, pushing Jillian's door open.

Jillian was perched on a big rubber yoga ball, reading an academic journal while she rubbed a hand over her bulging belly. She smiled beatifically. "Hi, Charlotte, did Sonja send some sort of childbirth emergency text? Because I'm fine. I swear it was just a little heartburn after my lunchtime pie."

"Jillian! Charlotte has a small favor to ask. Would you mind sharing a little bit of the baby's eggshell after the birth?" Sonja asked.

Jillian removed her reading glasses, which Charlotte suspected were more for familiarity than for correction. Phoenix eyesight was damn near perfect. "Are you going to do weird science experiments with it?"

"Why is that everybody's go-to?" Charlotte asked, throwing her hands in the air. "Do I have 'weird scientist' written on my forehead?"

"No, it's just an unusual request." Jillian said.

"She's going to use it to try to lift the curse on Leonard," Sonja squealed. "It's so romantic! Curses and dragons and fairies. I freaking love living in Mystic Bayou."

"I never said it was a romantic thing!" Charlotte cried.

"Oh, that's just the nicest thing I've ever heard." Jillian needed help from Sonja to push her way into a standing position, but then flew at Charlotte to wrap her in a hug. Soon, Charlotte felt warm tears dripping down her neck. Jillian sniffed, wiping at her suddenly wet cheeks. "Yes, you can take as much of the shell as you need. Please remove the curse from Leonard. We love him, and we want him around for a long time."

"Great! Thanks—"

"What are you all talking about?" Leonard was standing in Jillian's open door, holding a bulk mail carton.

"Leonard!" Jillian sniffed. "Charlotte thinks maybe she can use my eggshell to remove the curse! You'd be so much safer! And freer! And just imagine the stress it would take off of you!"

Leonard shook his head, a wounded expression souring his normally handsome features. He turned to Charlotte. "I told you what could happen if I try anything to remove the curse. The time for Seamus to apologize is long past. This is just something my family has to live with."

"What happens if you try to remove the curse?" Sonja asked.

"It gets three times worse," Leonard growled, putting his hands on Jillian's desk. But his palms were sweaty and his hands slipped on the slick surface, throwing his weight off balance and sending him sprawling across the carpet.

"We did not know that," Jillian said, suddenly very calm and contrite.

"I never asked you to remove anything, Charlotte," he insisted as Sonja helped him to his feet. "And frankly, it's a little insulting that you think you have to 'fix me.'"

Bold words from a man previously sprawled across the carpet.

"I'm not trying to *fix* you, I'm just trying to remove an element that you didn't ask for that makes your life more difficult! OK, that does sound a lot like fixing," Charlotte said.

"I think we should excuse ourselves," Sonja said, curving her hand under Jillian's elbow and helping her waddle out of the room faster. "You two, just work this out in here."

She closed the door, leaving Charlotte to face the music. Or at least, a hurt and disappointed Leonard, which was a lot worse. And heaven help her, if Leonard was attractive in his normal state, seeing him all fired up like this? His eyes got brighter, more intense. The red cheeks and tousled hair gave him a sort of tragic hero aesthetic. She was suddenly very aware of just how much strength he had in that tall frame of his, given the size of that bulk mail carton. The man had hidden, hotter depths. If she could just crawl into his lap and explain things—

No. She should not be having these thoughts right now, while he was all agitated and angry with her in her boss' office. Right, she was in her boss' office. That helped.

"Charlotte, I didn't tell you any of that stuff about my family because I was trying to get you to do something about it," he said. "I told you that stuff so you would understand me better, so you would know me."

"I know that. I know you weren't angling for anything. But if there is a way to remove it, don't you think you should try?" Charlotte asked.

"I told you, it's not possible. It will only make things worse," Leonard said.

"My mother says that's not how curses are supposed to work," she assured him, kneeling in front of his chair to take his hands in hers. "If you can apply it, you can remove it."

"Well, pardon me if I'm not willing to literally bet my life on your mom's theories," Leonard said.

"So do you want to *stay* cursed?" she demanded.

"Of course not, I just want a choice in the matter!" Leonard exclaimed.

"That's what I'm trying to give you!" she cried.

"Great! Then we both get what we want!"

He ducked his head suddenly and kissed her hard. Her arms wrapped around his neck as a reflex and he was lifting her up into his lap—again, it was like she weighed nothing. As she straddled his hips, all the possibilities of Sonja's office chair became readily apparent. It would be wrong to strip him down entirely, she thought as she tugged at his sensible blue check tie. Nudity in Sonja's office would feel good, but would be very, very wrong. And it would destroy her career.

It would probably be worth it.

When Charlotte finally came up for air, she gasped. "Wait, what?"

He ran his hands through his hair and settled her to sit sidesaddle across his lap. "I want to remove the curse just as much as you do. Trust me. But I'm scared. I wouldn't be acting this way—all crazy—if I wasn't scared. So please, please explain what you're thinking."

Tucked against his chest, Charlotte recapped her conversation with her mother about the eggshell, the laws of curses, and the power of belief, and how it might have kept his family trapped over the years. Leonard shifted back in his chair, a series of horrified, frustrated, and heartbroken expressions cycling across his face. She kissed his forehead. "I'm so sorry."

"So if you're right, all of this time, we could have found a way out of it?" Leonard asked.

"Yes, but think of how much kinder and considerate your family has been over the generations because of the bad example of Uncle Seamus." Charlotte told him.

"It's pretty cold comfort," he muttered.

"Working this kind of magic is different than giving a baby a blessing," she sighed. "It's different than casting a curse. But I'm willing to try if you want it."

"What's it like? The blessings and the curses?" he asked quietly, toying with her hair. "What's it like to have that kind of power?"

"I don't really think about it much. The blessings are a bit like weaving. I have all of these threads of magic that I can feel in the air, and I chose the ones I want to bind together, to attach to people. The curse? Well, the one curse I cast? It was much more intentional. I wanted an *outcome*, not just a quality in a child that would be helpful to them in life. And afterwards...well, I won't lie and say it didn't make me feel better.

"Can you tell me about it?"

"It might change the way you feel about me," she said softly, toying with his shirt buttons.

"I can't promise it won't, but isn't it better to get everything out in the open?" he asked.

He stroked his hands down her back as she spilled her tale. "It was before I worked for the League. I did a short stint in a birthing center in the Midwest. It was a nice enough place to work but there was this office manager there, Dan. He was always a little too 'friendly' with my coworker, Zoe. It escalated really quickly, from a comment here and there about her appearance, to using her employee records to get her phone number and send her a proposition at 2 a.m."

"I feel like I should apologize on behalf of my gender," Leonard tucked her head under his chin. She felt *so* safe there. How could she feel so safe and settled when they'd been yelling at each other just moments before?

"So, *did* she report him?" he asked.

"She did everything she was supposed to. She kept a record of everything, took all of it to HR. She was willing to go to meetings where every single word she said and wrote was scrutinized while Dan stared her down from across the table. You would think that a medical center focused on women would have had comprehensive sexual harassment policy, but we didn't. And Dan knew just how to skirt that line of plausible deniability," Charlotte said.

"I was furious, but Zoe? She just sort of shrank into herself. She couldn't move or get another job. Her parents were older and they needed her close. So either she put up with his bullshit or she gave up the job she loved and all the time and training it took to get it. And the harassment wasn't stopping, because Dan knew he could get away with it."

"And you did something about it?" Leonard asked.

"I don't even remember making the decision. Like I said, blessings and curses aren't about rituals. It's more a matter of *will*. Something needed to happen to Dan, to make him understand the pain he'd put Zoe through, and it was like this moment of clarity inside of my head, where I willed it into being. He took Zoe's voice from her, so I took his voice from him."

He squeaked. "Permanently?"

She scoffed. "No, just whenever he tries to defend himself from an accusation. Even if he's innocent, he won't be able to say so. He won't even be able to write a defense. If he tries, it will just come across as nonsensical strings of letters."

"Oh, well, that doesn't sound so bad."

"Well, I also fixed it so anytime he thought about treating someone the way he treated Zoe, he would throw up until he managed to feel some remorse. But that only lasted a year," she admitted. "I think he learned faster than your ancestor."

Leonard shrank back. "Yikes."

"I know. It's bad. But I didn't make his entire line suffer. Just him. He was the one who deserved it."

"I can't say I approve, even if he did deserve it," Leonard noted.

"Yeah, and I'm OK with you not approving. I just want you to know that I wouldn't ever use it against you. I would never hurt you," Charlotte promised him.

He kissed her temple. "Let me think about the curse removal thing, OK? Maybe we should both take some time to just think about all of this. We're moving a little fast and maybe you should think about long term stuff, like whether you want to stay here in the Bayou, which is my plan for the near future, and whether you can live with my being cursed if I decide not to have it removed."

She opened her mouth to object and he held up a hand. "Let's both just do some thinking."

She nodded. "All right."

6

CHARLOTTE

*S*he woke to what felt like thunder rattling her trailer apart. She shot up in bed, checking her phone for missed calls or weather alerts, blearily registering the blows raining down on her door. It was only three a.m.

She'd only dropped off to sleep an hour or two before, stewing over her conversation with Leonard, and wondering if she'd managed to derail their relationship before it even started. The lack of sleep made her slow and stiff, so she was unprepared when Zed's voice boomed from outside, "Charlotte! Wake up, please! It's started!"

She stumbled to her door to find Zed, wide-eyed and shirtless, panting on her doorstep. If she was not such a loyal person–and not deeply afraid of what Dani could do with those lightning balls–she would be much more affected by the sight.

Zed shoved a travel cup of coffee at her. "Dani sent this."

"You remembered coffee for me, but not a shirt?" she asked, rubbing at her eyes.

"That was Dani," he said. "Bael called. Jillian's water hadn't broken. She's only had four contractions in the past hour. But in the middle of the contraction, she set her phone on fire. And then she set Bael's phone on fire while he was texting me. And then she set his laptop on fire. It was a rough day for electronics at their house."

"OK, so we don't need to panic. Everything is going just the way it should. Why didn't Jillian call me?" she asked, closing the door so she could slip on some jeans and shoes.

"The phones were all on fire," Zed reminded her.

"Right. You've got those fireproof suits at the cave, right?" she called, grabbing her medical kit and her go-bag, a phone charger, and her granny's journal.

"And the extinguishers," he yelled back, lowering his voice as she stepped out and locked the door. "Bael's already got her on the way out to the cave. I'll have to blindfold you to take you there. It's a dragon thing. Secret treasure hordes and rules and such."

She nodded and wrapped the bandana around her neck. "OK."

Zed's dark brows rose. "No objections?"

"Do you think that's the weirdest request I've ever gotten?" Charlotte asked.

Zed frowned. "Well, I *did*."

Zed managed to find a spare shirt behind his driver's seat. Charlotte climbed into the truck and tied the bandana tightly around her eyes. She could feel Zed making hand gestures in front of her face. He started the engine and drove out of town. She could feel the tension rolling off of his huge frame as he silently maneuvered the truck. He only spoke again once they'd parked in a dark wood that smelled of wet earth and decay.

"Do you mind if I invade your personal space a little bit?" he asked over the drone of nighttime insects. "It would be easier if I just carried you rather than asking you to go trip through the woods blindfolded."

"Sure," she said, shrugging. "I'll need my strength over the next few days."

He wrapped her around his back piggyback-style and carried her bags in either hand.

"I'm literally the only other person besides Jillian who knows where this is located. And that was only after Bael knew me for years and for safety purposes. He had a cousin that was crushed under some ancient Greek marble statue in his cave and no one found him for months because he left a series of very complicated maps and clues to find his cave. Bael didn't want to die in the dragon version of 'I've fallen and I can't get up.'"

She snickered into Zed's hair. She didn't have the heart to tell him that all *zana* had an infallible sense of direction. She knew her exact coordinates down to the nearest tenth, even blindfolded in the dark woods. It was necessary when your kind was expected to help lost children find their way in the forest. But Bael didn't need to know that. She'd never steal from him. And who could say no to a piggyback ride through the woods?

Zed seemed to calm down while walking through the woods, though he kept a brisk pace. Unlike the drive, he kept up a sort of stream-of-consciousness one-sided conversation talking about his lifelong friendship with Bael, what it was like to see his best friend fall in love when Bael had sworn to stay single his whole life, the hilarity of watching Jillian "hand him his own ass" on several occasions. It was nice, and Charlotte had almost fallen asleep against Zed's back when he finally stopped.

"All right, you can take off the blindfold," Zed said.

She loosened the bandana. They were standing outside a huge concrete structure made out to look like rocks, covered in vines and swamp plants. Several bonfires lit the enormous campsite outside the cave entrance. Bael had Jillian seated in a little camp chair while he carried boxes through a set of metal double doors set into the side of a concrete "cave."

"Hey," Jillian said, waving awkwardly. "Sorry about sending Zed to kidnap you."

"Oh, it's fine," Charlotte said, waving her off. She pulled her blood pressure cuff out of her bag and checked Jillian's vitals. "Everything looks good. How are the contractions?"

74

"They're maybe fourteen minutes apart. I told Bael we probably shouldn't call you yet, but then I set our phones on fire and freaked him out," Jillian said.

"It's fine. Better too early than too late," Charlotte assured her. She nodded to the moving boxes stacked near their chairs. "What is all this? Groceries?"

"Oh, Bael and Zed stocked the cave 'pantry' yesterday. This is books," Jillian said. "If I'm going to sit on a nest for days at a time, I'm going to need entertainment.

Charlotte nodded. "Sure."

"Is that a port-a-potty?" she asked of the green plastic structure placed fifty paces from the door.

"Yes, it is," Zed told her. "Good luck with that."

She sighed, pinching the bridge of her nose. "Well, it's not the roughest conditions I've ever worked in."

"Do I want to ask?" Jillian snickered.

Charlotte shook her head. "No, you do not."

Zed nodded towards an enormous plastic water tank nearby. "The good news is, with Bael around, there will always be hot water for you."

He lifted the lid of a nearby cooler to reveal carefully labelled containers of gumbo, cornbread, chicken and dumplings, and other comfort foods. "My *maman* cooked enough to keep you fed for a couple days. Some of it is labeled for when–before and after the birth–Jillian is supposed to eat it. To keep her strength up."

"May the Fates bless your *maman*," she sighed.

Zed nodded to another cooler. "And then Siobhan sent a whole case of what she called 'medicinal pies,'" he said, nodding to the smaller cooler. "And I'll make regular deliveries."

"Shit!" Jillian hissed in pain as another contraction hit. Her hair erupted into blue flames, crowning her like a nightmare queen. "Shit, shit, shit, shit, shit!"

Zed rushed to Jillian's side and took her hand. "Now, come on, *bebelle*, what was that whole thing about not introducing profanity to the womb? I've watched my mouth for months no-owwwwwwww!"

He howled in pain and dropped to his knees as Jillian squeezed his hand, breathing through the contraction.

"Ohhh! Zed, I'm so sorry and I love you very much, but stop making word sounds near me!" Jillian cried. Zed only whimpered in response.

"Deep breaths," Charlotte said, her voice firm as she placed her hands on Jillian's belly. The baby kicked inside, strong and sure. Everything was right on schedule...just painful.

Zed slowly and carefully pried his hand out of Jillian's, shaking the blood back into his fingers. He whimpered, "Ow."

"OK, let's move you onto your nest," Charlotte said. "Bael!"

Bael sped out of the cave and cradled Jillian into his arms, her blue flames spread over his body. He didn't even seem to notice, just carried her inside the cave, her blue light shining in the dark interior.

"Wow," Charlotte breathed, watching them with wide eyes.

"Yeah, I threw a bucket of water on them the first time I saw that. And then I did it again, just for fun," Zed told her.

"Your hand OK?" she asked.

He flexed his hand, grunting ruefully. "Don't tell Jillian, but I think I should go to Will's and make sure she didn't break anything. And maybe cry for a little bit."

"I've got my satellite phone. If I need you, I should be able to reach you," she said.

"I'll drop by every day, just to check in." Zed's eyes were almost misty as he eyed the cave door. But she couldn't tell if it was senti-ment or the throbbing of his potentially fractured fingers. "That woman means an awful lot to me. And Bael, I don't know what would happen to him if…. Please take care of them."

"I will," Charlotte promised, hugging him.

Zed closed the door behind her as she walked into the warm space with its strange musty, metallic smell. She was immediately overwhelmed by a sense of claustrophobia. She was a creature of the forest, of green growth and light. She was not meant to be kept underground. She shuddered as her footsteps echoed into a deep, concrete-lined void that stretched beyond what she could see.

Jillian had shifted into an enormous and brilliant blue bird, feathered in flames. She was settled onto a nest of glowing embers, her long swan-like neck tucked down as she breathed deeply.

Bael paused and casually blew out a lengthy line of flames that lit one and then a long line of torches stretching to the end of the cave. Torchlight reflected off of piles of gold–coins, platters, statues, chests of jewels–practically blinding her if she stared too long in one direction. It was all she could do not to run around the cave, shoving treasure into her pockets, fulfilling her *Goonies* fantasies. But she knew that she was already pushing Bael's instincts to their limits, she didn't want to test him further.

The fellas had obviously "swept" a significant corner of the cave, baring the floor to make room for two camping cots and a pile of pillows and blankets, multiple camping coolers, and an enormous rock fire circle already chock-full of lumber. In the far corner, in the darkest part of the clearing, he'd set up a privacy screen and a beaten copper bathtub.

"We tried to make it as comfortable for you as possible," Bael told her "Jillian's used to sleeping in a sort of nest of pillows at home, so I brought them–for afterwards."

"Do you need to take a break before we get started?" she asked. "Drink some water, get something to eat? Because your energy is a little...on edge."

"It's nothing personal. It's just a big thing to let a stranger into my treasure horde. Between that and trusting you with my mate and my young–that's an awful lot of trust I'm placing in you, Charlotte," Bael said.

"I know, and I appreciate that. You're going to do great, Bael,"

Charlotte promised him. "But can I ask–just one more time–that your dragon form try not to eat me?"

He rubbed his hand on the back of his neck. "If you could just keep reminding me that you're there to keep Jillian and the baby safe, that would help."

"I can do that. We've got this." She extended her hand, which he shook firmly. He crossed the cave, undressing in an unlit corner. Charlotte heard cracking and metallic shrieks while the shadows shifted and grew.

Bael was impressive in human form, but in dragon form, he was a magnificent nightmare made of fangs and scales. Her brain just couldn't seem to process a threat as large as a bus and she stood there, goggling at him like an idiot. His green and gold scales shimmered in the firelight in blinding patterns. He stretched his wings, the span rivalling that of most commercial jets and shook them out. While her hind brain was in a total panic, she couldn't help but think that he looked like an enormous dog shaking off water.

Bael curled his body around Jillian's nest, breathing in a sort of comforting huff. Jillian leaned forward and nuzzled her bronze beak against his snout. Charlotte sat on the bed, keeping vigil while the parents curled into each other and waited. She tried not to let Bael see her staring at his treasure, but every once in a while, some shiny piece would catch her eye–a jewel-encrusted comb, a silver shield engraved with the goddess Artemis, a sapphire the size of a mailbox. So she took lots of patient notes to keep her eyes on something else.

Jillian's contractions became more regular, if the shuddering and bursts of blue flame from her beak were any indication. She only got close every hour or so to check on Jillian (while wearing full fire gear). And even through the thick protective canvas, she could feel the heat radiating off of Bael's scales.

She tried to give Jillian as much privacy as possible as the egg, well, *emerged*. She hovered nearby as the great bird's body gave a final heaving shudder. Relieved of its burden, Jillian's fiery form sank against the coals, as if drawing the heat from them. Dragon-Bael bumped his nose against Jillian's side and then the egg, which was indeed metal and about three times the size of a football. The surface was scaled, in concentric patterns of shimmering blue and green. It was the most beautiful thing Charlotte had ever seen. She was afraid to touch it as Bael's massive form crept forward, nosing the egg into position under his own body.

The blue flames and feathers disappeared, leaving a naked and very sweaty Jillian on the cave floor. She smiled, laying a reverent hand on the egg. "Hey there, baby. It's Daddy's turn now, but I have all kinds of books to read you while you're waiting."

"Bael, just a reminder that I'm here for Jillian and the baby. It would be very bad manners to barbecue me," Charlotte said, covering Jillian quickly with a fireproof blanket before starting her usual exams. The new mother seemed to be in perfect health, other than being exhausted and sore.

Charlotte handed her a robe, which Jillian slipped into and slumped into Bael's side. He lowered his huge head to gently touch the top of her own. She laughed and kissed his snout.

Not for the first time, Charlotte felt like an intruder in a very intimate experience for this little family. She missed Leonard. Even though things were still unsettled between the two of them and she wasn't even sure if he would use the removal potion when she made it—she missed him desperately. She wanted to text him, to let him know she was thinking of him, that she'd slept badly the night before, worrying that she'd ruined a relationship that was only starting. But she figured, "taking some time to think" probably meant a break in communication. She didn't want to overstep again. But she missed feeling that growing connection between the two of them, the feeling of being understood, even when they disagreed. With seeing his face, her hours seemed just a little bit darker.

Of course, she was in a cave, which could have something to do with it.

She tried to give Jillian and Bael some privacy, disappearing into the shadows of the cave to fluff Jillian's "nest" of pillows Bael had prepared and dig into Zed's miracle coolers. She noticed a box marked, *Books for when Bael is playing penguin*.

Charlotte burst out laughing. "Because male penguins sit on the eggs, right?"

"Yes!" Jillian's face brightened and made grabby hands for the books. "You get me."

Charlotte eyed Dragon-Bael carefully as she passed Jillian the books. She held up a jar of dark golden broth swirled with flecks of sediment and bubbles of oil. "Apparently, Zed's *maman* swears by this bone broth, according to the label. She makes it for every new mother in the parish. You're supposed to sip it to restore all the stuff you just lost in labor."

Bael grumbled, constricting tighter around his family like the great reptile he was. They stayed, cuddled together like that, for what felt like hours, while Jillian sipped her broth and read from a book titled *Dragon Tales of Scandinavia*. A lot of the stories seemed to involve human heroes being tricked and eaten by the dragons, but Jillian's warm, gentle voice made them sound magical. Jillian read until Bael fell asleep and her own voice seemed to go hoarse.

"It just occurred to me why the egg is made out of metal," Jillian said, leaning into Bael's side. "It's so tiny compared to the dragon's body. It's way too easy to crush. This whole *magique* thing is just full of amazing little intricacies like that. It almost makes the world make sense. Ours, at least."

Jillian chuckled, finishing her broth. Charlotte helped her clean up as much as possible and got her settled onto the pillow nest. As she ventured outside, squinting into the too-bright sunlight, her cell phone pinged with all of the text messages and emails she'd missed while underground.

"These satellite phones have some serious reception," she told

Jillian, as she carried water back into the cave.

"Anything interesting?" Jillian asked.

"Just an email from my mom, which contains an ancient recipe for curse removal," Charlotte said, scrolling with her thumb. "And a reminder from Sonja that you're not supposed to ask for any news about what's happening back at the League office when you're supposed to be resting and recovering. She and Alex have everything covered."

Jillian pinched her lips together. "She doesn't know *everything* about me."

"There was a P.S. where Sonja said, 'And tell her, yes, I do know everything about her,'" Charlotte added.

"We're going to pretend that didn't happen," Jillian said, yawning and snuggling into the pillows. "In the interest of avoiding my control issues—we have some time. You can tell me all about your conversation with Leonard the other day."

Charlotte didn't look up from her phone. "I think asking me to tell you about a private conversation only proves Sonja's point about you having control issues."

"Do you *want* the eggshell when all this is over?" Jillian asked, brows raised.

"You're going to blackmail me in front of your baby?" Charlotte gasped, pointing to the egg.

"Fine, can you tell me about the recipe?" Jillian asked. "Or does that violate fairy-patient confidentiality?"

"Nah, that's not really a thing." Charlotte scanned the email, frowning at the intricate steps required with relatively common ingredients—besides the dragon's eggshell. "It doesn't look like it's going to be very difficult. I'll need the shell, moonwater, some quartz, earth that hasn't seen sunlight in at least nine years..."

Charlotte glanced pointedly at the dirt floor of the cave. "I could probably prepare it while we're here in the cave, if you don't mind me splitting my time in the first few days after the baby is hatched."

"No, it would be great if I could observe the process!" Jillian enthused.

"I'm going to have to put Bael in charge of your rest schedule on your maternity leave, I just know it. Oh, and the potion also requires that I wear a really big diamond tiara while putting it together," Charlotte asked, pointing to a particularly gaudy crown set jauntily on a golden stature of Horus.

Jillian patted Charlotte's head. "Nice try."

~

It took three days of Bael egg-sitting before the baby finally hatched, giving Jillian plenty of time to recover and Charlotte time to assemble her potion ingredients. They'd both started to lose track of time, only knowing a day had passed because Zed had stopped by to check on them. Jillian was huddled in her nest of pillows, making notes by the light of a lantern. Charlotte was pretending she *wasn't* looking at a solid gold bowl that appeared to be filled with emeralds the size of her fist.

And suddenly, the eggshell bowed outward, a strange metallic sound like a car door being ripped off of its hinge. Bael stirred, shaking his head back and forth. While Jillian bounded off the bed–fueled by Clarissa's comfort food–and ran across the cave, Charlotte approached the embers carefully. It was a strange sensation, not knowing what was going to be inside the egg. Would it be a small flaming bird? A tiny dragon? Or a baby human?

The suspense ended quickly enough when a tiny human fist jabbed through the shell, making Bael shuffle back. It was all so quiet, it was almost off-putting. There was no exultant and incensed howl as the baby left their mother's body. The egg simply broke and fell away, the bottom cradling a perfectly beautiful little person.

"Oh, look at her!" Jillian cried, tears trailing down her cheeks. "She's so beautiful, Bael! Just look!"

"I'm going to examine baby as quickly as I can," she told Jillian, watching the dragon, whose head was hovering over them, sniffing. "Bael, I'm just going to check her vitals and then I'll get out of the way, OK? No biting. No fire. OK?"

Dragon-Bael snorted. She took that as a non-verbal contract and peered into the shell. Inside was the most beautiful little girl that Charlotte had ever seen, with bright golden hair and a little rosebud mouth. Her head was perfectly rounded and her amber eyes alert. Charlotte did her assessments as quickly as she could, touching the baby as little as possible with her bare skin so Jillian's would be the first scent and touch the baby knew.

"She's as healthy as can be," Charlotte promised. When Jillian lifted her up from her cozy little shell, the baby burst into indignant tears. A little circle of blue flames ignited from her hair, making Jillian coo, "Oh, baby, it's OK."

The baby's hair was on fire.

That was something Charlotte hadn't seen before.

Bael shrank back into his human form, throwing on a pair of sweatpants. He knelt beside his wife, the most heart-breaking expression of joy and awe on his face. "Do you think that's going to happen every time she cries?"

"Most of the nursery has been fireproofed anyway," Jillian said. She took the baby to her breast to nurse, wreathed in blue flames.

Bael turned his attention to Charlotte, speaking softly. "Thank you."

"You two did most of the work," she said, waving him off.

"What's her name?" Charlotte asked. When the parents stared at her, confused, she added, "For the blessing."

"Really?" Jillian squeaked.

"That's the job, deliver the babies and give them the gifts they need," Charlotte assured her. "And yes, I know a dragon's name is serious business. Her true name never leaves this cave."

Bael leaned close to his daughter and whispered the baby's name against her little forehead.

Charlotte giggled. "Dalinda Zedwin Melrissa Ramsay-Boone, I grant you the gift of kindness, so that all that know you may love you, and of hope, to maintain you during the darkest hours," Charlotte said, her magic gathering in a series of silver threads, stretching from her hands to the baby's heart. Jillian sniffled. "And strength, so that all that love you, know to fear you a little bit, too."

"That's a good one," Bael sniffed, his eyes suspiciously wet. He turned to his wife. "Are we sure about the name?"

"Dalinda means noble serpent," Jillian said. "It's perfect."

"It's more of the Zedwin thing. Maybe we should make *that* the secret dragon name we don't tell anybody, instead of Melrissa," Bael said.

"Zed will be heartbroken if we don't name her after him," Jillian chided him. She turned to Charlotte. "Take all of the shell. Try to help as many people as you can."

Charlotte picked up the remnants of the eggshell, watching the torchlight dance across its iridescent surface. And she realized that her first thought was, "I can't wait to tell Leonard all about it."

That was what she was missing all this time, she supposed. Someone to share this strange life with. Someone who got it. Leonard was all that and more. And even if he decided not to use the potion, she would keep sharing this life with him, as long as he wanted.

Her mother was never going to let her hear the end of it, making her home so far away. But Lizzie and Hank could come and visit. And hell, if the economic boom was really coming to Mystic Bayou, maybe they could even stay in a hotel, instead of crowding into the Silver Stork with her. That would be a nice change.

But first, she had to help Leonard. Charlotte carried the shell to the little "lab" station she'd set up near her cot and went to work.

7

LEONARD

*L*eonard found that despite only knowing her for a short time, Mystic Bayou just wasn't the same without Charlotte around.

He was plenty busy. With Jillian gone, Sonja had more than enough work to keep him occupied during the day. Instead of sleeping, in his after-dinner hours he found himself wanting to call Charlotte, to tell her about his day or ask for updates on the wonderful and strange birth story. But he'd been the one to ask for this "time apart to think"–like an idiot–and now he had to do the responsible thing and really examine his feelings about Charlotte and the curse and her offer and...a bunch of stuff he probably wasn't mature enough to manage.

He knew he was wrong to get angry at Charlotte for offering to remove the curse. He was just thankful he hadn't lashed out any broader than he had. Fear could do stupid and destructive things to people, and he'd almost fallen victim. He thought maybe he wasn't even angry at Charlotte for meddling. Maybe it was the idea that she made this offer and it might not even work–like the possibility of false hope was enough to make him snap? The idea of being able to move and speak and hell, *dance* without the weight of the curse on his shoulders? It made him ache with want so bad he couldn't breathe. Charlotte was offering him a whole new life. And if it didn't work–even if the curse wasn't made exponentially worse–it might just break him.

But even if it didn't work, he had a feeling Charlotte would still be there. She hadn't been the least put-off by the curse or its side-effects. As long as she wasn't put off by his occasionally acting like a jackass, they might have a bright future together.

"Leonard, you doin' all right?" Zed asked.

"Yeah, sure, why?" Leonard responded absently.

"Because in all the time you've worked here, you've never so much as stepped in this building." Zed told him.

Leonard looked up and realized that he'd wandered into the parish hall, a large multi-purpose space where the various departments–finance, public works, everything else–were simply desks in one room. How he hadn't heard the constant ringing of phones around him, he had no idea. Zed and Bael were the only public employees to have their own offices, and that had more to do with the confidentiality of the information they handled than any prestige. He supposed that would all change, with the increased funding and other concerns heading into the town. And part of that made him sort of sad. A big part of the charm of Mystic Bayou was how the people did things their own way.

But this was not the time to think about population growth and culture change. Because the Mayor was staring at him warily. And it wasn't wise to provoke a wary mayor that could shift into a bear.

Charlotte had to come back soon. These were not the thoughts of a normal, functional adult man. Zed motioned for Leonard to follow him into his office.

"I am just worried about Jillian," Leonard insisted. "She's my boss and she really worked to make me comfortable here, instead of sending me back to DC for being a human disaster. And I just hope she's doing OK."

"So it has nothing to do with the little midwife?" Zed asked.

Leonard sputtered, "No, why would you ask that?"

Zed's dark brow lifted as a smirk formed on his face that sent a shudder of foreboding through Leonard's bowels. "That's OK. I think she made dinner plans with Jon for when she gets out anyway."

His head whipped toward the door as if he was going to run through the town and then the woods to get to Charlotte before Jon could put his...flippers on her. Leonard sprang to his feet, his feet tangling with the edge of Zed's carpet and he fell over his chair, narrowly missing the corner of the Oaken desk hitting his temple.

"Aha!" Zed thundered. "I knew you liked her!"

Leonard slumped in his strange prone position over the chair, defeated. "Well, of course, I *like* her. She's amazing, and beautiful and smart and capable. I more than *like* her. I would very much like to date her and eventually love her and have what you and Dani and Bael and Jillian have."

"So what's the problem?" Zed asked.

"I'm not sure." Leonard shrugged. "I'm cursed, and generally people who are cursed don't get what they want in life. That's sort of the point. So, I'm scared. I'm scared of being cursed forever. I'm scared of *not* being cursed and what that could mean for the rest of my life. And yes, maybe I'm a little scared of the idea of being with a woman who has the power to curse me *again* if things go sour."

"*S'il te plait*, do you think it's easy, dating a girl who can do what Dani does?" Zed scoffed. "You've seen her tase Adam McTeague with her *brain* during committee meetings when he waffles on too long, right? You think I'm not terrified? Most women who are worth the effort of relationships and all the pitfalls involved with them should scare you a little bit."

"You make a good point," Leonard agreed, scrubbing his hand over his face.

"So remove your head from your own ass and tell that girl how you feel before you lose her," Zed told him. "And that's the extent of my mature and manly advice."

They both jumped when a shrill noise sounded from inside the Oaken desk.

"What's that?" Leonard asked.

Zed whispered, "The Sonja phone."

He took the small red smartphone out of desk drawer and checked the screen. "It says '*Baby is here! Meet us at the rift site.*'"

A moment later, the phone chirped again and Zed added, "*And bring Leonard.*"

"How did she know I was here?" Leonard asked.

"It's Sonja." Zed shrugged. "How does Sonja know anything?"

"I'll get to see Charlotte," Leonard whispered. "I'll get to see the baby! Oh, holy hell, how am I supposed to get out of this room without tripping and knocking myself unconscious on office equipment?"

"I could carry you?" Zed suggested.

"Thanks, but no," Leonard grumbled.

Now the rift site was just an empty field near the Afarpiece Swamp, it was perfectly safe to meet the new family there. Zed drove carefully on the gravel road the League had installed to make it easier to reach the site, which would eventually serve as the new storage facility Cordelia and Brendan were setting up. Sonja's SUV was parked near the clearing, and Leonard spotted Will and Sonja waiting there with a tired-looking Jillian and Bael. Charlotte was leaning against a tree, watching the little scene while she sipped a bottle of water. Sonja was holding a little bundle wrapped in a yellow blanket while Will pressed a stethoscope against the baby's chest.

Apparently, the baby did not appreciate the intrusion of this cold metal object because Sonja startled suddenly and the bundle burst into bright blue flames. Bael stepped in, taking the flaming blanket from Sonja's hands while Will looked his girlfriend over for burns.

"Is the baby on fire?" Leonard asked.

Zed nodded slowly. "Yup."

"Things that only make sense in Mystic Bayou," Leonard sighed as they climbed out of the truck.

They edged closer, while the flames slowly died out and the baby's cries were replaced with burbling. Sonja laughed, cooing at the little bundle. "No harm, no foul, sweetie. We'll work out some sort of early baby flame warning system."

"Is it a boy or a girl?" Zed asked. "Or a bird? Is it something with wings?"

"Zed, meet your honorary niece, Dalinda *Zedwin* Boone." Jillian laughed as Bael handed the baby over.

"She's so tiny and perfect," Zed breathed, his hands trembling a bit as he held her. He stroked a finger down her little cheek. "Hello, sweet *bebelle*. I'm your uncle Zed. I will protect you and love you and do all the fun things that *maman* and papa say no to.... Oh, no, Bael, you've got a girl! You're never gonna sleep again! By the time she's ready to date, you'll be in jail for threatening any boy that comes near her. Oh, *merde*, that means I'm gonna be in jail, too. I'm gonna be charged with *accessory* to threatening any boy that comes near her. I can't let you go to jail alone."

"Her godfather, ladies and gentleman," Bael sighed.

Charlotte waved at Leonard, then motioned towards the waterline. "Let's give them a moment."

"How are you?" he asked, taking her in his arms. She relaxed against him, letting him squeeze her tight.

"Tired. Camping in the dark with a two-day-old is not for wimps," she confessed. "And we're going to go back to the cave for a few more days to let them all rest up a bit more. They just wanted to give Will a chance to examine her and to let her godparents meet her."

He leaned down and kissed her cheeks. "I'm sorry again, for how I reacted to your offer. I've had a chance to think about it, and I want all of it. The potion. The curse taken away. A chance with you. I hope you feel the same way, otherwise, I have screwed up in a major way."

"You're sure?"

He nodded. "Living your life in fear is no way to live."

She pulled a large mason jar from her shoulder bag. It was filled with silvery blue liquid, the consistency of dish soap. "Good, then I can give you this."

All of his hopes and dreams, the hopes and dreams of every O'Donnell in the last two hundred years—swirling around in a mason jar. He nodded, taking a deep breath before unscrewing the lid. "All right then."

"No!" she cried before he could lift the jar to his lips. "You don't drink it!"

"Well, how does it work?" Leonard asked.

"You have to bathe in it," she said. "And I have to be nearby."

"Well, I do have an awfully nice shower in my trailer," he offered, grinning at her.

"Actually, it will work better if you bathe in a *natural* body of water," she replied, grimacing as she gestured toward the murky brown swamp water.

"Oh, come on, there's nothing natural about that. I'll get eaten by alligators! Or worse, the Beasleys will see my junk!" Leonard said.

"Curse removal is also not for wimps," she said. "It's part of the reason we asked you to meet us here. I'll be here the whole time."

"And the rest of them?" Leonard asked, nodding toward the others.

"Having well-wishers nearby will also help," she promised.

"This isn't revenge because I acted like a horse's ass in Sonja's office?" he asked, stripping down to his underwear.

"Maybe." Charlotte made an innocent face that did not seem at all sincere.

"What is happening?" Zed asked.

Jillian and Sonja shushed him, while turning their backs to Leonard's impending nudity.

"Why is Leonard getting naked?!" Zed demanded as Leonard stepped into the surprisingly warm Bayou waters.

"All nude, O'Donnell," she reminded him. "I'll turn my back, too, if you want."

He sighed. "Nope. You're gonna see it eventually."

She wiggled her eyebrows. "Am I, now?"

"I've got plans, lady." He dropped his drawers and her eyes went wide as she handed him the jar. He tossed the boxers at her.

"Thoughts?" he asked, smirking at her.

"Um, I've just never dated anyone so...tall, before," she said, clearing her throat. Charlotte tugged at her collar. "Dunk your head under the water and start soaping up from your head and work your way, um, down. You're not going to get a lather or anything, so don't worry. It's working."

He ducked under the dirty water that smelled of fish and pennies, then took the lid off the jar. The contents smelled considerably better, like jasmine and a little bit like Charlotte. He rubbed the blue liquid into his hair, then scrubbed it over his face and neck. He could feel tiny chunks of metal in the "soap" and he could only assume that was bits of dragon egg. He felt a rush of love and gratitude towards Jillian, for giving up something that meant so much to her. He paused every once in a while to scoop more liquid out of the jar and onto his body. He could feel her magic washing over his skin, like warm, clean bathwater, leeching what was wrong from his being. It was like something in him that he didn't even know was broken, healed over. He felt whole and right and grateful.

"Duck under the water again," she told him. And when he raised up from the water, she handed him a towel. "Now comes the hard part. You can't bathe until the next new moon, which is in two days. It's kind of like Tupperware, you're trying to lock in the freshness."

"Well, I guess it's a good thing the blue stuff smells nice," he said as the others clapped and whistled. "And I'll be able to shower before you get back."

"I'm counting on it," she said, leaning up on her tiptoes to kiss him. He folded those long arms around her, and they stood there on the edge of the water, the weight of the curse easing away like some burden he'd already forgotten. He wanted to run. He wanted to *dance*. He wanted the next two days to be over so Charlotte could spend some much-deserved time off in his trailer.

"Can you do anything for the rest of my family?" he asked.

"Sure, Jillian said to use as much of the shell as I wanted. She would rather it be put to good use than sit in a baby memento box," Charlotte said.

"Would the same stuff work for Jessica?" he asked.

"I hadn't thought about it," she said. "Since that's curse work on a more divine level, I'm not sure it would work, but I can look into it."

"Do you have to?" he muttered into her hair.

She lightly slapped at his chest. "That's not very nice."

"Neither is Jessica," Leonard replied.

8

CHARLOTTE

*C*harlotte walked down the hall at the clinic, whistling. Things were very right in her world. Baby Dalinda was thriving and Jillian was recovering nicely. Mrs. Agarwal was due any minute now. And Leonard was celebrating his newfound grace in lots of interesting ways. They hadn't quite worked up to the most interesting and *bendy* experiments, but they were getting there.

Jessica was not pleased by this development. Leonard being less cautious in the office meant his work performance was even better. But Leonard's family was planning a sort of reunion in the Bayou so Charlotte could try to administer the "curse bath" for them as well. She was trying to determine whether she wanted to invite her parents down at the same time and just get all of the "getting to know you" awkwardness out of the way at once. That seemed like a lot to try to accomplish over one weekend.

Will had an early morning house call involving Emily McAinsley, so it was up to Charlotte to open the clinic that morning. She passed through the clinic waiting room to turn the "open" sign on the front door. She jumped at the sight of Dani sitting in the lobby, looking pale and somewhat miserable. Zed was standing over her, wringing his hands as he tried to get her to drink a bottle of water.

"Do I even want to know how you got in?" Charlotte asked.

Zed didn't even look sorry. "I broke your door. Where the hell is Will? We have an appointment with him in forty minutes and he's nowhere in sight."

"I'm fine," Dani objected. "I just can't keep anything down."

Charlotte crossed her arms. It appeared that the day of reckoning had come.

"Hey, Dani. How you doing, hon?"

"I just can't seem to shake this bug I've picked up. I thought it was food poisoning, but it's lasted for weeks," Dani said softly, rubbing at her stomach.

"I think it's something else," Zed insisted. "Like 'I can't believe I didn't pick up on the signs when Jillian just gave birth in a cave' something else. But Dani refuses to pee on the stick."

"Because I'm not pregnant, Zed, so keep your pee sticks to yourself!" she told him, much more firmly.

"Um, Dani, I'm pretty sure you *are* pregnant. I don't need you to pee on the sticks. I just know. It's a fairy thing," Charlotte said.

"But we used birth control, so much birth control." Dani's face went white, then red. She smiled broadly as tears rolled down her cheeks.

"Sometimes shifter biology likes to make a mockery of modern contraceptives," Charlotte told her.

"It's not going to come out in a big metal egg, is it?" Zed asked, rubbing Dani's back.

"I'm pretty sure that was a Jillian-specific thing," Charlotte assured him.

"I'm so happy!" he shouted, kissing a still-sniffling Dani. "But if Jillian threw up lava, what is Dani gonna throw up? Lightning?"

"The lava was also a Jillian-specific thing...though lightning vomit would be really interesting," Charlotte mused.

"I think I would rather the baby take after you and avoid electric morning sickness all together," Dani sniffed. "Even if it means giving birth to a small grizzly."

"Or maybe it will be an electric bear!" Zed mused making Dani's eyes go wide in panic. He tucked a dazed Dani into his side. "Life in the Bayou, eh?"

Charlotte grinned at him. "Well, it's not going to be boring."

ABOUT THE AUTHOR

Molly Harper is the author of more than thirty paranormal and contemporary romance, women's fiction, and young adult titles, including the Half-Moon Hollow series, the Southern Eclectic series, the Sorcery and Society series, and the Audible Original Mystic Bayou series. Molly lives in Michigan with her family.

Be sure to check out https://www.misscastwells.com/ for more information on the Houses, when the next book in the Sorcery and Society series is coming out, and fun fan goodies.

Where to find Molly
Website: https://www.mollyharper.com/
Twitter: @mollyharperauth

photo credit: J NASH PHOTOGRAPHY

ALSO BY MOLLY HARPER

all lists are in reading order

The Southern Eclectic Series (contemporary women's fiction)
Save a Truck, Ride a Redneck (prequel novella)
Sweet Tea and Sympathy
Peachy Flippin' Keen (novella)
Ain't She a Peach?
Gimme Some Sugar

The Mystic Bayou Series (paranormal romance)
How to Date Your Dragon
Love and Other Wild Things
Even Tree Nymphs Get the Blues
Selkies Are a Girl's Best Friend
Always Be My Banshee
One Fine Fae
Shifters in the Night

The "Sorcery and Society" Series (young adult historical fantasy)
Changeling
Fledgling
Calling

The "Nice Girls" Series (paranormal romance)
Nice Girls Don't Have Fangs
Nice Girls Don't Date Dead Men

Nice Girls Don't Live Forever

Nice Girls Don't Bite Their Neighbors

Half-Moon Hollow Series (paranormal romance)

The Care and Feeding of Stray Vampires

Driving Mr. Dead

Undead Sublet (A story in The Undead in My Bed anthology)

A Witch's Handbook of Kisses and Curses

I'm Dreaming of an Undead Christmas

The Dangers of Dating a Rebound Vampire

The Single Undead Moms Club

Fangs for the Memories

Where the Wild Things Bite

Big Vamp on Campus

Accidental Sire

Peace, Blood and Understanding

Nice Werewolves Don't Bite Vampires

The "Naked Werewolf" Series (paranormal romance)

How to Flirt with a Naked Werewolf

The Art of Seducing a Naked Werewolf

How to Run with a Naked Werewolf

The "Bluegrass" Series (contemporary romance)

My Bluegrass Baby

Rhythm and Bluegrass

Snow Falling on Bluegrass

Standalone Titles

And One Last Thing

Better Homes and Hauntings

CPSIA information can be obtained
at www.ICGtesting.com
Printed in the USA
LVHW010227280821
696293LV00006B/1183